# N.I.M.R.O

Ann Halam was born and raised in Manchester, and after graduating from Sussex University spent some years travelling throughout South East Asia. She now lives in Brighton with her husband and son. As well as being a children's author, Ann Halam writes adult science fiction and fantasy books, as Gwyneth Jones.

# The
# N.I.M.R.O.D.
# Conspiracy

## ANN HALAM

Dolphin Paperbacks

First published in Great Britain in 1999
as a Dolphin paperback
by Orion Children's Books
a division of the Orion Publishing Group Ltd
Orion House
5 Upper St Martin's Lane
London WC2H 9EA

A catalogue record for this book
is available from the British Library

Typeset by Deltatype Ltd, Birkenhead, Merseyside

Printed and bound in Great Britain by
Clays Ltd, St Ives plc

ISBN 1 85881 677 7

# One

*I* WAS WITH MO, IN THE FIZZY DRINKS WE WERE blocking half the aisle, unloading stacks of own-brand cola. (Yes, you're right. We *do* put stuff in your way just to slow you down. All part of our cunning plan to part the customers from their money.) It was a Saturday morning in May. Countryfare was stuffed with Saturday profiles: Dads with harrassed expressions and tiny babies fastened to their fronts doing the bulk shopping, Mums with lists, toddlers running about underfoot, a few young singles buying fancy beer and chill-cabinet meals, a few early tourists.

Anyway, we were talking about UFOs.

It's always coming up, isn't it. Lights in the sky, glowing craft glimpsed by airline pilots, unexplained explosions in the atmosphere, Americans getting mean medical things done to them on board a flying saucer: and the bottom line is that the aliens are amongst us. Living on earth already. Mo didn't think there was anything in it.

No little green men, that is.

'It's natural phenomena,' he said. 'Lights in the sky, big bangs, all natural phenomena. You ought to read the science pages. It's meteorites –'

'But there's usually no craters –'

'– that burn up before they hit the ground. Or melt. A lot of meteorites are lumps of ice.'

'But supposing it *is* aliens, come to invade and take over the earth –'

'What if they don't want to take over?' said Mo,

changing tack to confuse me. 'What if they're just looking for a place to stay, room to move in? Then what do we do?'

'Send them down the Jobcentre,' I said, grinning at the thought of a big rush of little green men and women scanning the boards for vacancies. Part-time, temporary, unskilled aliens –'

It was a game we played, chewing over the topics of the day, each of us trying to top the other in instant-expert opinions.

'Excuse me,' said a pleasant voice. 'Could you tell me where they've hidden the shampoo?'

Mo and I rolled our eyes at each other. Here we go again.

If we like a person, we give them a straight answer.

If they're rude, we give them a lot of directions that will take them on an extensive tour around the stacks. And they might find what they're looking for, by the way.

I stood up. I'd been on my knees when she spoke, shoving cola bottles onto the lowest shelf. There was a woman standing there, mid twenties maybe. She was fairly thin, medium height, pale-skinned, wearing jeans, a white sweater and a white baseball cap. You couldn't see her hair. She was wearing dark glasses, the kind that react to the sun. Under the store lights they'd cleared to the colour of smoke, but you still couldn't say much about her eyes. She was wearing silver earrings like coiled-up snail shells: like ammonites, those fossil things. She was smiling.

I recognized her at once. There was no confusion, no doubt, only a huge shock, as if someone had poured a bucket of icy water over my head. Or as if a wave had broken over me, a great, cold, roaring, salt-tasting wave.

'Well –' I said.

She gave a little nod. Just for me. So that I would know I was right.

'I'll show you.'

I couldn't look at Mo. I just led her away. I don't know how I managed to walk straight. After so long, after years –

At the end of the aisle I spotted Big Liz, our supervisor – the one who was after me to get sorted, do some exams, move on to the Countryfare fast track. She was holding a clipboard and obviously looking for someone. I suddenly recalled that a few moments ago I'd heard my name on the PA. This was the morning I was supposed to be doing another of those shopper-profile surveys, or some other daft exercise in Retail and Distribution Performance Measurement.

'Just walk this way, madam.' I did a swift dodge into own-brand frozen desserts.

'This doesn't look much like shampoo,' she said, still smiling.

'You should try tasting some of them.' But I'd had enough of that enigmatic smile. I had to know what was happening. Was I hallucinating, or had the past really torn open again?

'You were there, weren't you?' I blurted out. 'You were there, that day.'

And she nodded: very firmly this time. 'Yes. It was me.'

'So what's going on? What are you doing here? Why didn't you – ?'

'This isn't a good place to explain.'

Three years ago, this woman (if it really was her) had witnessed a tragedy. She had never come forward to tell her story at the time when it might have saved me. Now, out of nowhere, here she was: the person who could tell me the answer to a most terrible question. The person who knew what had really happened, on that day when my life stalled for ever. She was right, it wasn't a good place to explain anything. Shoppers were barging around us, the noise level seemed to have risen to dizzying heights.

'Look,' she said, 'can we meet? When do you get off work today?'

'At six.'

'Okay, come over here.' She led me across the front of Cheese and Dairy and pointed through the scrum of shoppers round the check-out lines, through the plate glass of Countryfare's frontage to the world outside. 'See that pub on the corner of the car park, the Queen Victoria? I'll be waiting outside at six p.m. this evening.'

I was too stunned to react. By the time I'd gathered my wits, she had vanished in the crowd.

# *Two*

*T*HREE YEARS AGO . . . IT WAS THREE YEARS AGO, AT the end of May; in half-term week. The day before had been my cousin Rosa's birthday. She was six. My little sister Stacey, aged five, had been at the party and had stayed the night. My Aunt Sara – my mother's sister – lived in Seastead, a smaller resort about three miles along the coast from Beachcombe, the big seaside town where I live. About lunchtime on the day after the party my mother, who was a teleworker for a finance company, gave me some money and told me to go and fetch Stacey. My father and mother were separated. They were in the middle of getting a divorce, though I didn't know the details about that: I didn't know how far things had gone. I was thirteen. I went over on the bus to Seastead, I picked up Stacey from my aunt's. On our way back to the bus stop we took a diversion through the shopping centre. I started playing video games in a small arcade there. I had some money of my own and that was all I meant to spend. But one thing led to another and soon we were penniless.

I could have gone back to Auntie Sara's and told her what I'd done, but I didn't like her much and I didn't want to get told off. I could have phoned home. I'd heard of reversed charges, but I didn't know how to do it. And I didn't want to get into trouble. I decided that we would walk back to Beachcombe along the shore. I didn't know anything about tides. I mean, I knew that tides go up and down, but I'd never looked at a tide table and I probably wouldn't have understood one if I had. So we went down to the beach and we set off. It wasn't easy to get her going. Our Stacey could be a little monster, and when I told her we had to walk home she threw a huge tantrum. But once I weathered the storm, it was okay. It was good. She was a great kid when she wasn't screaming and kicking. The gap between our ages meant I'd never once thought of her as a rival or an enemy. I didn't have to look after her too often, and she wasn't old enough to follow me around and be a nuisance. So we got on well. It was a hot, sunny afternoon. We took our shoes and socks off and paddled in those long, slippery strands of rock pools, under the chalk cliffs that stand along the Beachcombe coast. We shared the birthday cake and the sweeties from her party bag. We looked for shells and sea anemones and shrimps. And the tide came in.

I suppose we'd been going about a mile when I realized that we actually *couldn't* turn back, not without swimming for it, because there was now a deepish inlet between us and the beach at Seastead. And we couldn't get up the cliffs either. And that the three miles back to Beachcombe, which was nothing much to me, was an awful long way for a five-year-old.

A little bit later I realized that I had to tell her I was frightened, because otherwise she wouldn't have the sense to get a move on. A little bit later again, there was no longer any need to explain why we should be frightened. The sea had caught up with us. We had to cross another inlet, and we were going to get wet. There was a small pier there, I remember, for fishermen or something: and some rusty ironwork among the rocks. I had both our pairs of trainers, with the socks inside, tied by the laces and hung round my neck. I had her bag with her overnight things in it on my back. I decided the rest of our clothes would have to take their chance. I started to walk across. Before we were halfway the sea was whooshing around my waist, Stacey clinging on to me and kicking (she couldn't actually swim). The sun was warm, the water was calm and the sea was every shade of turquoise blue in the distance, sand-brown where it lapped around us. I had to swim for a bit in the middle, which was very scary, but I never lost my nerve: and we got through. I was so proud of her. She was being absolutely brilliant, our Stacey.

After that inlet there was no more beach. We were on the sea defences: those piles of great grey concrete knucklebones, like dinosaur vertebrae, that you see massed in heaps along our coastline, to protect the base of the cliffs from storm erosion (I think). I put her shoes and socks back on, and mine too. This part was slow going because Stacey was tired, and her little legs couldn't stride from bone to bone. I tried carrying her, with the overnight bag slung on my front, but that was no good because I couldn't keep my balance. So we had to clamber along, using our hands, like ants crawling across a pile of gravel. But I didn't mind the slowness too much because I thought we were okay. I thought we were nearly safe.

There had been plenty of people on the front at Seastead, but for a long time we'd been completely alone. When we'd been clambering along the sea defences for a while, I spotted a lone sunbather. This gave me a big lift. If he's down here, I thought, it must be okay. He must know he isn't going to get drowned. I watched this little patch of colour, a bag and a towel with a body on it, getting closer, feeling better all the time; although by now the sea was lapping halfway up the knucklebone heap, and we were being pushed closer and closer to the sheer cliff.

By the time we got level with the sunbather I could see Beachcombe beach along the horizon, beyond the next bend. I could see the esplanade and the pier, and cars and people. It looked as if we were saved. It looked as if there'd be no need for anyone to know that Stacey and I had been in trouble. So I played it cool, and when this woman (it was a woman, not a man) sat up and looked at us, I just waved. She had a little mobile phone by her hand, I noticed: which would have come in useful . . . We clambered on. When we came to that last bend we were following a sort of path of scuff marks, footprints and sand along the top layer of knucklebones, right against the cliff face. At the corner I got a horrible shock. *There was another inlet.* The knucklebones around it were already under water. Water lay twinkling wide and blue and dark, between us and safety. It looked as if there was no way across bar swimming. And the tide was still coming in.

I'd spent my whole life in Beachcombe, but I lived up in the town. The beach was just another tourist attraction as far as I was concerned. I'd never explored along the shore. I didn't know anything. I'd had no idea this inlet would be in our way. On the other side of it a forest of masts bobbed gently, poking up from behind the massive wall of the Marina.

I knew I couldn't swim across there, not with Stacey hanging on to me. I'm terrified of deep water, always have been.

'What are we going to do?' asked Stacey.

She didn't sound too frightened. I suppose she trusted me.

'We're going to ask that sunbather. She must know the way.'

So we clambered back the way we'd come. It seemed to take a horribly long time. She stood up when she saw us coming: a slim young woman in sunglasses with a white baseball cap that covered all her hair. The sun glinted on her silver earrings. She was wearing a white bikini. Her fair skin was still quite pale. She must have only just started cultivating her tan. It didn't cross my mind to wonder what she was doing there all by herself, I was too worried.

'Can you help us?' I asked, trying to sound calm.

'We've been caught by the tide, and the path seems to give up, along there.' I pointed.

'Of course.' She smiled, what a wonderful smile. 'I know the last bit looks tricky, but it isn't. All you have to do is go on, around the corner. There's a little path up to the top of the cliffs. It's easy.' She looked at Stacey. 'Don't worry, you'll be able to do it too.'

I looked at the mobile phone. I thought, well, if Stace *can't* do the last bit, we're still okay.

'She was nice, wasn't she,' said Stacey happily, as we set off again.

'Yeah, very nice.'

'I like that lady. I think she's our friend. She's very pretty, isn't she.'

'Yeah, very pretty.'

I was thirteen, tall and skinny, with a face I was going to have to grow into, all nose and jaw: a long drink of lumpy water, my Auntie Sara used to say. I didn't have much success with girls my own age, but I had an imagination. The sunbather was gorgeous, obviously a loner, and she had smiled at me. I had a whole romance worked out before we got back to the point where the path seemed to disappear.

When we reached there, I put my shoes on. I settled Stacey with her back against the cliff, on a flat place where two bones lay fitted together: sitting down, perfectly safe. Our new friend was in clear sight, down below. I waved to her again. I ordered Stacey not to move, and went to look around the corner. The escape route was there: easy as walking upstairs. It was about ten or fifteen metres to the top of the cliff. I shot up there, and in what felt like less than a minute I was on the grass, by the clifftop path. Cars were zooming along on the road that passes the Marina. On the other side of the road, I could see golfers on the golf course. Down below me a big motor yacht was passing, white against the blue. The little bunch of rocks that people called 'The Islands' was glittering on the horizon, with a cloud of seabirds' wings flashing around it. On the clifftop no one was about. It was a lonely sort of place, though it was so near the town: nothing moving but the pink flowers in the turf that were sitting in the sea breeze. I stood there just breathing, glad to be alive. It's quite something, to have been in real danger of death by drowning . . . I yelled, I cheered. I turned a few cartwheels. Then I headed back to get Stacey.

All the edge of that clifftop looked the same. It took me a minute or two to find the path down again, but it couldn't have been more than that. I wasn't away more than five minutes, maybe ten at the absolute most, before I got back to where I'd left her.

She wasn't there.

That's the end of the story, really. That's when my life ended.

But just for the record:

I couldn't believe she'd fallen into the water. It wasn't as if I'd left her on a tiny ledge or something, she'd been sitting on a big piece of solid flat stone. But that's the first place I looked for her. I flung myself, scrambling and falling, right to the brink of that dark blue, glittering blank. I'm scared of deep water, but I'd have jumped in if I'd seen any sign of her. I couldn't. I clambered along, to and fro, yelling her name, scanning the surface of the sea. Then I climbed up again, and up to that corner again, and up the cliff, in case she'd followed me and somehow got to the top without me seeing her. No Stacey. I scrambled down again to where I'd left her, still shouting her name; and oh, how my heart was thumping, how every moment I was convinced that the horror would end and she would be *there*, she would reappear, I would hear her crying from somewhere where she had fallen. It seemed to go on and on for ever. It was as if I was fighting to wake up from a nightmare but at the same time I knew this wasn't a nightmare, *no, it wasn't a dream*, it was really happening, something more terrible than I had ever imagined, and it would never be over . . .

The young woman who had been sunbathing was gone too, though she hadn't passed me. When I noticed this I felt terribly betrayed. I had been so sure that Stacey was safe, because there was a grown-up, my gorgeous sunbather, close at hand. But I didn't wonder how she'd managed to disappear. I was in too much of a panic.

· In the end I had to give up. I went home and told my mother that I'd been standing at the bus stop with Stacey in Seastead, and a man in a car had pulled up, and grabbed her and driven away with her. My clothes were dry by that time, and in her panic she didn't notice anything suspicious. I stuck to this story for weeks afterwards. No one could shake me.

I don't know why I did it. *I couldn't help myself.* I knew that what had happened was my fault because I'd spent our bus fares, and I didn't want to get into trouble. The fact that Stacey was gone, and I was responsible, and I was making things worse by not telling the truth, was something my mind couldn't cope with.

At first what I most hoped and most feared was that her body would be washed up and the truth would come out. As the days went by and this didn't happen, I didn't even know that I was lying any longer. It got so I could see it all in my mind: that dead stretch of road where the bus stop is in Seastead. The retired people's seaside bungalows, and their gardens silent in the middle of a hot sunny afternoon. The man, the car, Stacey screaming as she was dragged away. Me, yelling and running and spending futile time searching for her . . .

No sign of Stacey was ever found, then or later.

About four weeks after she'd disappeared someone came back from holiday, heard about Stacey (the police were still appealing for witnesses) and recalled seeing a young boy answering to my description down on Seastead beach that afternoon, dragging along a little girl who was screaming and struggling. He identified me and he identified Stacey, from photographs. He was a very good witness. So the police came back to our house. They found my crumpled salt-stained clothes and Stacey's overnight bag where I had hidden them in my secret place under a loose floorboard in my bedroom. Mum hadn't noticed the clothes were missing, but she identified the things I'd been wearing that day.

And I broke down.

I told them what had really happened. I said I'd lost our bus fares (*even then*, I wouldn't say I'd spent the money) and we'd tried to walk home and we'd got caught by the tide. I described exactly how Stacey had disappeared. I told them about the sunbather, I even told them about the motor yacht, in case somebody on board might have seen me and Stacey. They questioned me and questioned me, the police and my parents, and the social workers. I told them every single thing that I remembered. I was afraid I was going to get accused of murder and put in prison, but it didn't come to that: just endless questions until I thought I was going mad. I suppose they were all trying to understand why, if I was innocent, I had told so many lies: why I'd kept up my false story so convincingly and for so long.

No sunbather came forward. The investigation slowly closed down, without a result. And that's how it ended: without an ending. Terrible questioning, terrible suspicions, no sign of Stacey. Stacey gone for ever, the police losing interest, my little sister neither dead nor alive.

Naturally, the disappearance of a little girl had been in the papers and on the TV. When the real story came out, a couple of the tabloids decided to make something of it and printed some really sicko suggestions about what might have happened after I dragged my little sister off 'screaming and struggling'. We (I mean my parents) got the law on them and they shut up, but of course people at my school had been reading all about it. I don't think

Mum knew how bad things were for me, afterwards. I couldn't tell her: not when it was all my fault. I just kept my head down and endured. I left after my GCSEs, with the nearest thing to no qualifications. When I was sixteen and three months, I left the college where I was supposedly studying and took a shelf-filler job at Countryfare. It got me out of the house.

So this was my life. Going nowhere. Just waiting to die.

After she'd walked away, I went to find Mo and we went on stacking shelves. He knew there was something up, but he didn't ask questions. Mo was my best mate at Countryfare. He was about forty, I suppose. It was hard to tell, because of the way he was disabled. The left-hand side of his face was scrunched up, and he had no ear on that side. He limped a bit and his left hand was clumsy, and it was hard to understand what he was saying until you got used to it. We probably looked like an odd pair, but he was a really good floor worker. That was why I was put with him on my first day, and somehow we had hit it off. We had the same sort of minds, the same sense of humour. And Mo's kind. He just looked at me that first day, saw this big husky gangling youth towering over him: and he knew I was in small, shattered pieces inside. He'd watched out for me ever since. He covered for me the rest of that morning, while I wandered in a daze, hardly able to find my way around.

I struggled on until about three o'clock. Then I went to find Liz. I told her I had a cracking headache and I was going to have to go home early. She said I looked like death and I must be getting the flu, and gave me a couple of paracetamols.

In the staff room – a room like a glorified broom cupboard, lined with lockers and coat-rails – I got myself a coffee from the machine in the corner and sat holding it, full of conflicting thoughts. My memories of that afternoon were so clear. I remembered tiny details, like the sunbather's smile, her silver earrings. Yet how could I be sure, after three years . . . ? And yet, it *must* be her. Why would she be claiming to be my sunbather, if she wasn't? But why had she turned up now? After so long? The questions and possible answers kept running around in my head, but only one thing mattered. If she was my sunbather, she knew the truth. From where she had been lying, in her nook among the stone knucklebones, *she had to have seen what happened to Stacey.*

For three long years (a lot of that time spent at school, where some people thought maybe I really *did* drag my little sister off to a secluded spot, to rape her and kill her) I'd been clinging to the knowledge that there was *one person in the world* who knew the whole truth and knew for certain that I had done nothing terrible. I'd been stupid, I'd been childish: but at the moment when Stacey actually vanished *it wasn't my fault.*

When she fell –

I stared at the wall of lockers in front of me. It was too late, it had always been too late. For three years I'd been hanging on to a pathetic, cowardly illusion. There was no one who could tell me that I wasn't to blame. What could my lost witness say? Whatever she told me would be too much and not enough. It wouldn't bring Stacey back.

I swallowed the paracetamol. I don't know why, I didn't have a headache. I poured the rest of the coffee down a sink in the toilets, put my bright green Countryfare nylon coat in my locker; then I went home.

# Three

*H*ERE'S WHERE WE USED TO LIVE, AN ORDINARY house on an ordinary street. Alan and baby Stacey and Mum and Dad, and a black-and-white cat called Bono. Here's our front garden, with the lawn where Alan and Dad used to play football. Bono is buried in one of those flower borders, having died at a comfortable old age, not much bothered by the tragedy that destroyed the rest of us. I walk up to our front door, which is painted the same bright red as always. The same curtains are in the windows. Nothing changes . . .

My dad moved right away, with his new girlfriend, after the investigation. Before Stacey vanished he had talked to me about him and Mum splitting up, and they had both promised me it would make no difference. Stacey and I would live with Mum but he would still be our dad, he would always be nearby. But he couldn't stand the Stacey business. I think most of all he couldn't stand the way Mum kept on hoping. That's the way it goes. A tragedy like a lost child pulls other things down with it, like a house of cards falling apart.

So everything changed. But now, inside this house, nothing changes . . .

I let myself in. Mum called: 'Is that you, Alan? You're home early.'

'Yeah. I had a stinking headache. Going to lie down for a while.'

She was in her office, that used to be called the dining room when Alan and Stacey lived here with Mum and

Dad; a room I called the Stacey Robarts Operations Centre. That was where my mum spent her life, sitting in front of her computer keyboard or working among her piles of papers: checking mailing lists, writing letters and answering them.

Mum used to have career plans. She was working part-time at home while Stacey was little, but she'd meant to get better qualifications and go back to work with her old company. She'd had to give all that up. She could only work a few hours a week these days. She needed the rest of her time to keep up with the search. The walls in our former dining room were covered with pinboard, stuck all over with messages, postcards, sympathetic letters, digitized photographs showing what Stacey might look like now. Maps from all over the world showed reported sightings of children who might be Stacey marked with coloured pins. There were photocopied articles about missing persons agencies, the relevant bits striped with highlighter . . . None of the leads she'd followed had ever come to anything, of course. But there were always more of them. I'd given up hoping that Mum would ever accept the truth.

She didn't come out to say hello. Although we lived together, Mum and I didn't see much of each other. She was only happy (if you could call it that) in that room; whereas I hated to walk through the door.

I went upstairs. In a moment I would be in my bedroom: safe. To get there I had to pass the door of Stacey's room. It was open. Always open. Stacey didn't like you to shut her door, day or night. I hardly need to tell you that nothing had been changed in there since the day she disappeared. Everything was kept clean and tidy, but otherwise untouched: same heap of soft toys, same picture book open on her little desk. The only thing that was missing was the purple plastic home of Torquil the cyberpet. Goodness knows where she got that name from, but Torquil was my sister's top toy when she vanished.

The pathetic tunes it played, and the cheeping noises it made to attract attention, used to drive me crazy. Torquil had generally spent his off-duty hours hanging on a hook by her pillow. But he must have been in the pocket of Stacey's shorts, the day she . . .

I'm sick of saying it.

I looked into the room. I couldn't stop myself, although I knew what I would see. As I walked up the stairs I'd felt the strange creeping in the air, like cloying, invisible fingers brushing my skin, that always warned me. She was sitting on the bed, dressed in those blue shorts with the yellow daisies on them, and the white T-shirt with the cartoon baby dolphin, and the yellow cotton hooded jacket with the zip fastening, open at the front. Her yellow hair was hanging down her back in damp, darkened strands, her bare feet were pink and wet. She was playing with Torquil. I could hear his tinny little tune.

She looked up. She looked at me with eyes as blank and dead as stones.

'Hi, Alan.'

I pushed myself past the door. Into my own room. Sat on my own bed, with my temples suddenly pounding. There was that headache. I'd wished it on myself.

I had been seeing my sister's ghost for three years. Not every day, not even every week, just *sometimes*. I ought to be used to it by now. But it never got any better, never. It was no use telling myself that there was nothing to be scared of, that she never *did* anything, that she didn't even look horrible, no bloated skin, no rotting flesh, nothing like that. I just felt terrible, terrible, terrible, every time. Sometimes I pleaded with her to leave me in peace, but she didn't seem to hear.

My lost sister, come back to punish me.

No one else could see her. I knew this because she didn't mind appearing when Mum was around. I'd seen Mum look straight at my little ghost, without a flicker of recognition, and I was sure she was not faking.

Maybe the worst thing about the way I was haunted was that my mum would give her soul to see what I saw, or to hear that little voice again: and I knew she never would. That was one reason, one very good reason why I couldn't tell her what kept happening to me. I'd never told anyone, in fact. There was no point.

On my way home I'd been half wishing I'd had the courage to keep that appointment and let the lost witness tell me the truth at last. But how could I have any doubt about what she would say? A child too frightened even to scream, a little girl scrabbling and falling, into the deep . . . I'd imagined it so often. Mum could go on believing, but how could I doubt that she was dead, when I was haunted by my little sister's ghost?

It would be really interesting, I thought bitterly, to know why my sunbather didn't *do* anything when she saw Stacey fall into the sea. And how she disappeared the way she did, and why she never came forward later on . . . Maybe she'd been on a long, long vacation. The moment Stacey and I turned our backs, maybe she'd rolled up her towel, put away her mobile phone and dived into the sea with her waterproof beach bag tied round her neck. Swum out to that motor yacht, took ship for South America. Just got back . . .

No. The more I thought about it, the more pointless a meeting seemed. I didn't need anyone to clear my name, because I'd never been accused of a crime. And Mum was happier, if you could call it that, while she could pretend she didn't know the answer to the only question that mattered. It was better this way. Me with my little ghost, Mum with her everlasting support groups and mailing lists, just carrying on.

# Four

SHE DIDN'T TURN UP AGAIN. I LOOKED OUT FOR HER in the store, and I kept an eye on the Queen Victoria. When I came off work I'd leave by the back entrance, then sneak round and look at the front of the pub from across the street: but she was never there. If she knew my home address or phone number she didn't make use of them. I'd have thought I'd imagined the whole thing, except that Mo had been there. After a few days I told myself she couldn't have been my sunbather. The whole thing was just a strange little mystery, or a misunderstanding, that meant nothing. I put the incident out of my mind.

But I think I knew, secretly, that it wouldn't stop there. Someone, for some reason, had tossed a pebble into the dead pool that was my life, and the ripples must spread . . .

A week after she appeared something else happened. Mum told me one of her 'net friends' was coming to visit and wanted to meet me. Mum was a keen cyberspace user. The global computer network is full of information about anything and everything, and 'Missing Persons' is no exception. There was a whole culture of desperate people like Mum online, all signed up to the same newsgroups where they could read messages about missing persons – rumours, news, cries for help, tales of miraculous reunions, tales of sad endings, all kinds of stuff. Mum had made a lot of contacts like this. She had 'net friends' in the missing persons club all over the world. They sent us Christmas greetings and holiday postcards. They didn't often turn up on the doorstep: but it could happen.

I didn't want to meet this woman. I didn't have anything against her, I'd have felt the same about anyone connected with the search for Stacey. However, Mum had specially asked her round on a Wednesday afternoon, which was the day I got off work early, so I couldn't easily get out of it. When I let myself in I heard voices from the Operations Centre. I stood and listened, not exactly eavesdropping but trying to work out what kind of person the visitor was. It was a woman's voice, but deep and husky . . . Mum opened the door and caught me.

'Alan, there you are. I've just been telling – Come on, take your jacket off, come in, say hello –' She hustled me into the Stacey Operations Centre.

The woman I saw, sitting on our shabby leather couch, was much older than I'd expected. Not Mum's age at all. She didn't look like a computer nut. She looked much more like the kind of flashy old lady you might see in the saloon bar of one of the big pubs on Beachcombe seafront, with a large gin and tonic in one hand and too much make-up.

'This is my son, Alan,' Mum said. 'Alan, fold yourself up and sit down, don't stand there like a lamppost looking as if you're about to run away. Get yourself a cup. Have a cup of tea. Have a biscuit. No, don't sit over there, sit here. Pull your chair closer. Move those papers. This lady is here to tell us about something very important.'

My mum was like this whenever we chanced to meet, these days. She'd give me five or six orders at once, maybe in the hope that one of them would pin me down. I sat on the edge of one of the old dining-room chairs, but I didn't bother with the rest. I wasn't planning to stay.

'Oh, *Alan*,' said my mum. I suppose because I wasn't

looking very enthusiastic. 'At least *listen*. Dittany has very good news for us. She's moored in the Marina –'.

'Hello, Alan,' said our visitor, in her husky croak: a smoker's voice, I thought. She was wearing an African print thing, a kaftan, over white slacks, and a lot of gold jewellery. I noticed that her black bird's-nest hairdo was growing out white at the roots.

Mum was sitting at her work-station desk, with her chair turned around. The smile on her thin face was so bright it would break your heart. Good news, I thought. Oh no.

My worst suspicions were confirmed. I hated times like this, when some new 'evidence' would turn up, and Mum would insist on roping me in to listen to the story: or to stare at some blurry photograph of a little girl who might be our Stace, or read the letter from New Zealand, or whatever it was. She always said she wanted my *honest opinion*. Of course she didn't. She wanted me to say *Yeah! This could be it!*

Over and over again.

'So you're moored in the Marina,' I said to our visitor. 'Is "Dittany" the name of your boat?' I was trying to ward off the moment when we had to talk about Stacey.

'No, that's the name I took when I started working for NIMROD,' she said, in a matter-of-fact tone of voice. 'Colonel Proctor likes us to use our spirit names whenever we're on NIMROD business, whether or not we are working on the spiritual plane. Those who have gone astray may be listening, though we can't hear or see them.'

'Dittany needs to talk to you,' broke in my mum. 'About that day . . . from the moment when you were at the bus stop, and the man stopped in his car.'

I winced. This was another reason why I *hated* meeting 'Search For Stacey' contacts. My mum believed I'd taken Stacey down to the beach, but she hung on to the idea that we'd been followed by a stranger that day. She was convinced the police had bullied and confused me into saying the 'man in the car' had never existed. I think she just couldn't believe I would have lied so persistently, about something so important. Also, hanging on to part of my first story made it easier to hope. If Stacey had been kidnapped, then she might be alive now. I had given up arguing about this long ago, but I never knew what to do when she talked about the 'man in the car' to other people.

'I'm sure she knows everything about us already.' I gave Dittany a suspicious look.

Some of the people who turned up with fresh leads were genuine. Some of them were chancers, who'd read up about Stacey on Mum's webpage or in the newspaper archives, and were out to trick us somehow: to make money out of our misery.

'*Please*, Alan. At least let Dittany explain. You owe me that, don't you?'

I gritted my teeth. There was no way I could ever make up for the harm I had done. I would have to go through the charade, and talk to this old bat politely . . . But then something struck me. Dittany had used the words *spiritual plane* and *spirits*.

A chill went up my spine. Mum had never yet doubted that her baby was still alive. No matter what you said, she would insist something strange had happened, something we didn't understand. Stacey had not been murdered, or her body would have been found. She had not fallen, not drowned. She had been snatched away –

'Wait a minute, did you say *spirits*? Does that mean you're saying Stacey's dead?'

Mum winced. 'Please, Alan.'

She wasn't shocked that I would say it. My mum was obsessed, but she wasn't crazy. She believed in Stacey's survival, but she understood why other people didn't.

'Now that I don't know,' said Dittany. Her harsh voice

was still completely matter-of-fact. 'That's what we have to find out.'

'You'd better explain the whole thing to him,' said Mum. 'Alan's very intelligent, he'll understand. He's a trainee manager with a big supermarket chain.'

My mum's fantasies weren't only about Stacey.

'As your mother already knows, Alan, I'm a member of a group called NIMROD. That's an acronym. It stands for Never-ending Investigation of Missing-persons, Recovered Or Discovered –' Dittany took out a folder from the big clutch bag that was standing by her. I sighed inwardly. I had been here before. It was always the same. The testimonials from satisfied customers, the sad attempt at a catchy product name, the gobbledegook jargon of impressive words. The old monster was going to sell us her Missing Persons Scheme. Like someone selling double-glazing.

'Nimrod was a mighty hunter,' interrupted my mum, eagerly. 'That's in the Bible.'

'Right,' said I. I had no idea if this was true, I'm not a great Bible reader. But it was my policy not to argue with anything when in the 'new lead' situation.

'That's it,' said Dittany. 'Nimrod was a mighty hunter. It was Colonel Proctor, our founder, who chose the name. He's very religious.' She passed me one of her folders. I saw that Mum had another of them. I looked at a photograph supposedly of this Colonel Proctor: a slab-faced bullet-headed bloke with a bristle haircut, dressed in US army uniform. There were some printed pages, and a bunch of photocopied letters and things. I leafed through this stuff, which was exactly the sort of thing I'd expected, while she told me how Colonel Samuel Proctor, a spiritualist by conviction, had made a great discovery while working on something very hush-hush about computers in Washington DC. There were several spiritualist groups operating in cyberspace. But the Colonel had gone one better, and found out that not all the 'spirit messages' that were turning up on computer screens in these Internet seances were from the dead. Some of them were from missing persons. The same problems that could lead a person to walk out and vanish could cause the spirit to wander from the normal plane of everyday life, and send out messages into the mystic aether. Drug addicts, alcoholics, people who'd lost their memory, or were deeply depressed, or mentally disturbed . . . Exactly the sort of person that could not be traced by any ordinary means, could be sending these messages. They didn't know they were doing it, but their unconscious minds were crying for help. And in some way as yet not understood by conventional science, these messages could be intercepted by specially talented computer-users: and used to identify and locate the senders.

'It could be a child,' whispered my mother, at this point. 'A *child* could be sending out messages like that, Alan! Not knowing what she's doing –'

I was feeling slightly sick. This was not the first time we'd been targeted by the nasty side of the missing persons world. But I didn't get used to it. What kind of person does it take, to think it's a great idea to cheat people like my mum?

'So where do you come in?' I asked the old lady coldly. 'What do you get out of this?'

'Dittany's a *channeller*,' explained Mum, reverently. I could see she was hooked. There was nothing I could do.

'I've always had a psychic gift,' said the old lady calmly. 'When my late husband was alive, I never made any use of it. Since he died, I've been drawn to spiritualist circles. I found out about Colonel Proctor's organization through a spiritualist newsgroup, and it seemed to me that I might be able to help.'

'But what do you *do*?'

'It's like automatic writing,' broke in Mum. 'But typing, not writing. The channellers, like Dittany, use their gift to set up a dialogue with the unconscious senders, via a chatsite on the Internet. Then the hunters use the information to locate the missing persons. It's all organized internationally. They have lots of resources –'

'Have you lost someone yourself?' I said to Dittany. 'D'you know what it feels like? Do you know how cruel it is, to pretend to give people hope when there isn't any?'

'Alan!' hissed Mum.

But Dittany wasn't worried. 'My dear husband loved to travel. That's how I got into computer networking, it's a great way to keep in touch with absent friends. Now he's gone, and I'm travelling on alone. But I know where my Frank's body is buried, and I know his spirit is happy in the Beyond. I suppose you could say I'm just a lonely old woman who needs something to do. I believe I have a duty to use my gift, to help people.'

'That sounds great. It'd better be a financial gift, because we're strapped. So I hope you're not going to charge us for this service.'

'*Alan!*'

From the way my mum blushed at this moment, I knew she'd already signed the cheque. I just hoped the subscription to NIMROD wasn't too horribly expensive.

Dittany smirked. As well she might. She probably had a major chunk of our next month's budget tucked away in that shoulder bag. 'Don't worry, Mrs Robarts. It's natural. Alan doesn't know me from Adam.' She laughed. 'Or Eve, I should say. He'll change his mind.'

Then, without warning, she fixed me with her dark, hooded, made-up eyes and began to do some *gestures* in the air. Her nails were painted with bright silver varnish. They flashed like metal claws while her knobbly old fingers zoomed through a swift hand-jive. It happened so quickly, this shift from hypocritical sympathy to strange hand-waving, that it was *weird*. It was as if she was taken over by something other than her brassy, ordinary self. But I had managed to keep my wits together, and I remembered about Nimrod being a hunter. I thought I could read the signs.

She looks for something, she spots it. She draws a bow: she shoots down her prey.

'Okay,' I said, 'I get it. So what are you shooting your arrows at?'

'Very good!' said Dittany. She turned to my mum. 'He's quick.'

'What's it all about?'

'You and your mother will need to learn the handsigns. In the virtual environment, that means on the computer screen, we are identified by our spirit names. When we meet each other in the real world, we use the signs.'

'Like freemasons or something? Doesn't that make you look daft? Why?'

'When you've practised, you'll find that you can make the signs so that *nobody* except another member of NIMROD would notice them. It's a way to preserve everybody's privacy. And it protects us from interlopers. We don't want the media sneaking into our meetings. Some NIMROD material is quite sensational. I don't want to raise your hopes, but you may find out for yourselves what I mean.'

The story was getting confused. What could be 'sensational' about fake computer messages? 'Let's get this straight. Your group called NIMROD somehow collects computer messages from missing persons, maybe living or maybe dead. And then the NIMROD hunters interrogate these lost souls, trying to find out who they are –'

'It's the *channellers* who do the dialogue,' corrected my mother, reproachfully. 'The hunters work in the field, tracking down the senders.'

'You've got to be kidding. My sister was *five*. She couldn't type. She could hardly write her name.'

'She isn't five,' whispered Mum. 'She's eight. Her hair is turning brown. Her nose isn't a button any more, and she's lost those chubby cheeks. She's tall for her age. She has that little cleft in her chin, like her dad. It makes her look boyish, she was always a tomboy. But she's getting so pretty . . .'

I thought of my sister the way I'd seen her last. With her hair still darkened by seawater, and her eyes like stones. I remembered the woman who had come to Countryfare, and I realized it would have been no use, even if I'd brought her home. I could bring her here, and have her say to Mum *I saw your little girl fall*. It would make no difference. Mum would still find a way. She would go on believing, and she would go on begging to be cheated by monsters like this Dittany. It was horrible. I couldn't stand any more.

I stood up. 'I'll be upstairs, Mum. Nice to meet you Mrs – er – Dittany.'

'Alan,' pleaded my mum. 'NIMROD is *different*!'

'We don't know,' said Dittany. 'We're not sure. There are so many messages. But we believe we *are* in contact with your loved one. A little girl, who calls herself Stacey, who has a brother called Alan. She talks about a cat called Bono, and another pet called Torquil. There's other things she says, too, about the life she remembers from before she vanished. But you're the ones who have to decide if this is *your* Stacey.'

'Oh, *Alan*,' sighed my poor mum, her voice trembling with hope.

*Dear Mum. I'm wedged in a hole under the sea defences, most of me has been eaten by the fishes. Love Stacey.*

'Does Jo know about this?' Jo was my mum's boyfriend. 'What does he think?'

'Jo thinks it's worth trying,' she said, triumphantly.

Then I escaped, although Dittany (who could see I was the weak link in her chain) tried hard to get me to stay. There was no sighting of Stacey's ghost today, I was glad of that. I sat on my bed waiting to hear Dittany leave, and wishing I'd taken longer to get home. The trouble with being a shelf-filler with a big zero for a social life, is that you can't pretend that you have anything important to do, when you want to get out of something.

# Five

MY MOTHER'S BOYFRIEND IS A POLICEMAN. They'd met when Stacey disappeared. Joachim Brennan hadn't been officially concerned with the case. What he did – it was something quite high up, about investigating big frauds – didn't involve searching for lost children. But a few years before our case his wife had died of cancer, leaving him alone with a little girl the same age as Stacey was when she vanished. He'd heard about Mum, and felt sympathetic, and he met her and talked to her. I don't know the details, but he'd ended up sort of counselling her: that's how the relationship started. Three years later they were going strong. I'd hated him at first, for taking the place of my real dad. But I'd come to like him and depend on him, and I got on with his daughter Caz, Charlotte that is: she was thirteen now.

Jo wanted them to get married. Mum wouldn't do that. She wouldn't consider making any big change in her life until Stacey was found. So we lived a kind of half and half existence, Mum spending Monday nights and alternate weekends round at Jo's house when he wasn't on police business: me and Caz joining them to eat and do something together at least one night every week. It was a settled routine. Jo Brennan was that kind of person: very fair, very methodical, but very tolerant. When he understood that Mum *had* to spend most of her days and nights plugged into the Search for Stacey, he'd simply made room for her obsession. He'd set out a ground plan: *this* time belongs to Stacey; *this* time belongs to me; *this* time belongs to you and me and Caz and Alan as a family. It worked, pretty well.

The ground plan didn't mean we couldn't see each other at other times. But I waited a few days before I went around to Jo's house, on my own, to ask him about the NIMROD thing. I didn't want Mum to know I was talking about her behind her back.

It was about eight o'clock when I got there, on a sunny evening. Caz was on her own. I knew this before I reached the front door, because of the incredible racket. I let myself in with my own key. She'd never have heard me. She was lying on the floor in their big living room, waving her legs in the air and singing – or yelling – along to some unbelievably loud rap music with a kickin' bass line. Her eyes were screwed up shut, she was punching the beat and generally flailing about like a hyperactive beetle stranded on its back. I walked over and switched the amplifier off.

Caz sat up, saw me and glared indignantly. 'Why did you do that?'

'You're going to be deaf before you're twenty.'

'Huh?' Caz was just thirteen. Being twenty was something she couldn't imagine.

'What are you doing down there, anyway? Is that some kind of anti-cellulite aerobics?'

'I'm *break-dancing*. I mean, I'm learning –'

'Oh, sorry, I thought you were a squashed beetle doing karaoke.'

'You don't know anything, you sad, strange person.'

I saw her furtively feeling the backs of her skinny thighs through her kappas.

'I haven't got cellulite! Have I?'

'I don't know. I've never seen you in a skirt. Where's Jo?'

'Still at the office, of course. Will you cook me my tea?'

Jo had spent years trying different arrangements with nannies and au pairs, but since she was twelve Caz had refused to have anyone in the house, except for my mum and the cleaner who came in occasionally. This did not mean she was a domesticated young homebody. It meant she hated having anyone but her dad tell her what to do. Mum and I tried not to interfere. It was up to Jo to keep her in order.

'Cook it yourself,' I said. 'And you'd better hurry up. If he gets home and you haven't had your tea he'll be mad. Have you done your homework?'

'Nanny, nanny, nanny.' She stuck her tongue out at me (she's so mature for her age). 'I'll dial a takeaway pizza. It's quicker.'

Then we heard Joachim's key in the lock.

He is a big man, square-shouldered and thick through the middle, but not fat: with a broad, pleasant face, brown eyes and black hair that would have been as curly as Caz's if he let it grow. For work he wore suits, big well-cut suits in smooth dark cloth, either dark blue or very dark grey, that told you instantly he was someone in authority. Even when he was less formal, he looked imposing. He beamed when he saw me, but when I said I wanted to talk about Mum and NIMROD he looked glum. We went into his study, leaving Caz still lying on the floor, now with a phone in her hand, talking ham and pineapple with anchovies. 'Teenagers!' I groaned (I felt that at sixteen I'd outgrown the title). 'Doesn't she make you feel old?'

'I never liked teenagers much when I was one,' growled Jo. I could believe it. He must always have been big, sober and thoughtful, even when he was a kid. 'She don't make me feel old, she makes me feel exasperated.' But he was grinning. He and Caz had terrible rows, but between times they got on fine.

Jo's study was like his suits: big, well-made and quiet. There were dark green curtains at the windows, and a soft Persian carpet with a muted pattern covered most of the floor. He had a powerful PC on his desk, and a nice music, TV and video system. Most of the walls were lined with bookcases, and the books weren't there for show. He read a lot. On one side of his desk stood a picture of his wife, young and smiling, and one of Caz, aged ten, in her karate suit. On the other side of the desk was a picture of my mum. There was none of me, because I hate having my photo taken, but I knew that in Jo's mind I was there. When I told him that Mum had said he thought this new scam 'was worth trying' I expected him to laugh. Mum was good at listening to what you had to say, but only hearing what she wanted to hear. He didn't. He rubbed his chin, and looked at me uncomfortably.

'Ah, NIMROD. So now you know about them, too. Alan, you know it's difficult for me with your mother . . . anything about Stacey.'

The police had failed to find her baby. And no matter how often I told her otherwise she still thought they had bullied me into making something like a false confession. For all sorts of reasons, the Stacey business was a dodgy topic between her and Jo.

'I know. But I'm worried about the money. She won't tell me how much she's paying for this NIMROD thing, so I know it's far too much. We're already broke –' We were always broke. Mum had savings, but they'd been eaten away by the Search for Stacey, and Dad had never been brilliant at keeping up his maintenance payments. Between her part-time job and my shelf-filler's wages, we could barely make ends meet. Jo winced. Mum absolutely refused to let him help us out with the bills, but he knew our situation, and I knew it pained him to see us scraping and struggling.

'Can't you investigate? Isn't what they're doing called fraud?'

He shook his head. 'Not my kind of fraud. People believe what they want to believe, there's no law against that. No, I'm afraid not.' He hesitated, and then explained. 'The fact is, Alan, I've already looked into this

— 32 —

NIMROD operation, as far as I can go. I think they're fairly harmless, and that's the best I can do for you.'

So I had to confess what was really bothering me. 'She wants me to join in,' I muttered. 'She wants me to go on-line and, like, *talk* to this supposed Stacey.'

'Maybe you should do what she asks.'

Then I was more than amazed. I was shocked.

'You can't be serious. You're kidding, please tell me you're kidding.'

He passed his hand over his cropped curly hair. 'Alan, NIMROD *is* different.'

I stared at him. 'That's what Mum said. Jo, they're all the same.'

'Not this time. Think about it. The NIMROD people have told your mother that sometimes these messages of theirs come from the Beyond. They've told her that Stacey may be dead. And Jackie has accepted the possibility. Now, do you see?'

Jackie was my mother's first name.

'I know my sister's dead,' I whispered. 'Jo, I can't. I just *can't*.'

He reached over the desk and took one of my hands, which had suddenly clenched itself into a fist. Jo knew nearly all there was to know about my part in what had happened. He knew about my guilt and my shame, and the horrible time I'd had. 'Yes,' he said, gently. 'Like you, I think there's no possible reason to doubt that your sister died by drowning three years ago. It's unusual, and very sad, that we never found her body. But think about it, Alan. This is the first time your mother has considered the idea that Stacey may be gone. That it may be possible to mourn, and move on.'

'Yeah,' I muttered. 'I see that, but –'

He gave my hand a little shake, let go and sat back. 'Alan, the NIMROD people may be every bit as bent as you think they are. I'm not suggesting otherwise. But they could still help your mum, despite themselves. That's why

I think you should go along with her. Do whatever she asks you to do.'

'I don't know if I can stick the idea.'

'Well, try to stick it.' His expression turned grim and sad. 'I'm quite an authority on bereavement, Alan. I've read a lot of stuff about the processes we have to go through when we lose someone. The final acceptance could be sudden, now your mum's made this step. It could happen in one of these NIMROD sessions: suddenly she will *know* that her baby is gone for ever. It would be good if someone she loves could be beside her at that moment, wouldn't it? It can't be me. Swallow your doubts, Alan. Be with her.'

They wanted me to stay and eat pizza and watch a video. I didn't feel hungry. I went home instead. I was puzzled by Jo's attitude. It seemed almost immoral to go along with a bunch of callous fakers, even in a good cause. And I thought there was a flaw in his argument. Couldn't Mum get just as obsessed about staying in touch with a Stacey in the spirit world? In which case NIMROD would have their hooks in us for life. Still, I trusted Jo. So I knew I ought to give his suggestion a trial.

Next day, Caz told me that in fact her dad and my mum had had a blazing row about NIMROD. We were in Countryfare. Caz used to come in after school sometimes to chat: the store was on her way home. I had mixed feelings about this habit . . . Anyway, there she was in the biggest black nylon puffa jacket, with A for Anarchy scrawled in white marker on the back, black cycle shorts and monster trainers; jumping up and down and telling me her dad had been as suspicious as I was about NIMROD. She was trying to touch the topmost tin on a huge stack of backed beans –

'So what changed his mind? He told me I should co-operate. Sit by her when she's reading these messages and so on. Pretend to join in. But I can't go through with it.'

'Why not?'

'You know I hate computers.'

'It's easy, Alan. I've done it masses of times. You log on to one of these chatsite addresses and sit there in front of the screen. If you want, you can type in a message of your own, and get chatting. No one knows who you are, it doesn't matter if you make a mistake, you can say what you like ... But you don't have to do anything, you can just read the messages from other people. NIMROD can't be that different. Why don't you try it? You might find yourself talking to someone dead famous, I mean dead and famous. Or missing and famous ... What's the problem? Hey, why don't I do it for you?'

To Caz the idea of having a secret password to a weird website was thrilling. She was always messing around with her own computer – and getting into trouble for using her dad's, which was much fancier, when he hadn't said she could.

'No way. You stay out of this.'

'I don't know what's wrong with you. You don't have to believe in this NIMROD thing, you only have to go along with it for your mum's sake.'

'I can't explain.'

My mum had a NIMROD password now. I didn't know what it was. I wouldn't let her tell me. I wouldn't let her talk to me about what went on in the on-line 'channelling sessions'.

The top tin on the stack quivered dangerously –

'I DID IT! Did you see? I totally moved the highest one. Can you do it? Go on, try!'

'Of course I can do it, you stupid kid. I'm nearly a metre eighty tall. Look, what I want to know is: if they had a row about it, what made him change his mind?'

Caz came and perched herself on the edge of the frozen-food bin I was clearing out. She gave me her best withering smile. 'Can't you guess? He loves her. He wants her to marry him, and she won't say yes. My poor dad is finally cracking up. He'd do practically anything –' She grinned callously, but then she looked more serious. 'I think he's right. You should play along. Then your mum will really believe she's talked to dead Stacey, because she trusts you. Stacey will say, *I am so happy here in heaven*, and all that. Your mum will give up the search. They'll get married, you'll both come and live with us. It would be great to have everything settled, wouldn't it? Come on, Alan. Say you'll do it.'

As if it could be that simple. I almost laughed, but the wistful tone in her voice struck a nerve, reminding me I wasn't the only one whose life was stuck in limbo.

I hated being made to feel guilty by Caz as well.

'Why don't you just *lay off*?'

So she left, in a huff. I was sorry, but I couldn't do what they wanted. Just couldn't.


May turned into June, and there was a new development. Dittany revealed that there were meetings Mum could go to: private NIMROD gatherings where you could only get in if you did the handsigns at the door. There was a group that held its meetings in Beachcombe itself, where Mum could meet her fellow subscribers. This was good. It meant I could make a compromise. I could go along with Mum, wait outside, and be there to meet her when she came out. Not a very enthusiastic kind of support, but it was the best I could manage.

The first time I went with her it was to a pub on the seafront, where NIMROD had hired a room upstairs. Second time it was in the function room behind a busy Middle Eastern restaurant near the railway station. Third time it was a private house, out in the leafy suburbs. Mum would make those handsigns at the door, and disappear. I would hang around outside. The pub and the restaurant were okay, because they were in town. The house in the suburbs was more of a problem. I was lucky it was summer and the weather was fine. I wandered up and down the tree-lined streets, feeling a bit of a fool and probably looking like a burglar casing the joints. I had no idea what went on at these things. I wouldn't ask: and Mum, who was on her dignity about my attitude, didn't volunteer any information. We went to the places and came back more or less in silence.

The meetings weren't regular. It wasn't like every second Tuesday evening. It was more a case of mum getting a computer message or a phone call, and being told the new address, and when to come along. I supposed that was part of the impression NIMROD wanted to make. Like a secret society. Anyway, Mum seemed satisfied . . . except with the way I was behaving.

I had not forgotten my lost witness. That unexplained visitation from the past was in the back of my mind, though of course I didn't connect her appearance at Countryfare with a dodgy missing persons agency. But I had noticed things, like the red car (which I'll explain later), which made me curious. Then Mo said something that really started me thinking.

We were in the fresh meat, slapping free-range ducklings on to the cool-cabinet shelves. We were talking about premonitions. I was saying there was nothing in it. Mo was telling me about a friend of his who had a dream in which he lost money on a horse race, and a week later he put money on this horse . . .

'And the horse lost,' I finished for him. 'That's not even interesting, Mo. That's *not spooky.*'

I looked over his shoulder, and saw that old witch Dittany crossing the aisle at the end of the chill cabinets. I was horrified. What on earth was she doing here?

'Mo,' I hissed. 'Sorry, but I've got to get out of here –'

I grabbed a cold flabby lump of clingwrapped poultry in each hand, held them up on either side of my head and headed for the staff exit, stooping to conceal my height. The last I saw she was standing in the fizzy drinks, her rat's nest of black hair moving slowly to and fro as she scanned the crowds: like a snake about to strike. She scared me, that woman.

After a few minutes Mo came to find me.

'Were you hiding from the smart old lady with the big hair and the silver nails?'

'Yeah, I was. How d'you know?'

'She was asking after you. Knew your name and all. Don't worry, I didn't let on. I told her it was your day off.' Mo would rarely ask me a personal question, but of course he was interested. 'I bet she was looking for you the other day, when she was in here. When she made your girlfriend scoot. What have you two been getting up to, Al? D'you owe the old lady money?'

'Who do you mean, my girlfriend?' I demanded. Still holding the ducklings, I was peering out into the store, making sure the coast was clear. 'You don't mean *Caz*?'

'Nah, not the kid sister. The one in the sunglasses . . . Nice looker. the one who came up to us that Saturday, and you went off with her to the frozen desserts.' He looked at me curiously, screwing up his lopsided face. 'The last time *she* was in, she saw that flash old lady and she ducked out of sight immediately. Dodged into wines and spirits and exited very rapidly through an empty check-out . . . I was watching the whole thing. So what's going on? Are you two in bother?'

Mo and I were great people-watchers. When we weren't discussing current affairs or the paranormal, strange shoppers and their peculiar behaviour was our favourite topic.

'She's not my girlfriend,' I said. 'The old bat's a friend of my mother's. I don't know about the other one, never spoke to her except that once.'

I changed the subject. We went back to talking about slow horses in dream flat-racing previews, and people who incredibly turned out to have the same birthday as someone they met at the dentist. But I could see Mo wasn't satisfied – and neither was I. Dittany and my lost witness, both lurking around Countryfare . . . It was too much of a coincidence.

I had a strong, almost eerie sense of *things coming together*. A stone had been dropped into the dead pool of my life: and then another stone.

Now the ripples began to mesh –

When I got in from work Mum was in the kitchen, unusually. She was sitting by the breakfast counter with a mug of tea in her hands, staring through the window at our back garden. There wasn't much to look at. Dad had been the gardener. Mum and I kept the lawn mowed, but the rest of it was a weed patch. I stood and looked at her: first time maybe that I'd *looked* at her in ages. My mum didn't bother much with her appearance. Not even for Jo's benefit, recently. She wasn't wearing make-up and her hair – which was long and blondish-brown, the way Stacey's 'would be' by now – was pulled back casually in a ponytail. She looked too young to be my mother: and far too young for the years of sorrow in her eyes. I thought how lonely we were, the two of us, separated by the very thing that we most shared: my sister Stacey. Our lives would be so much better if I could bring myself to be a bit more understanding. I promised myself that I would try. Things would change. But before I did anything else, I was going to sort out the NIMROD business.

As I stood there making good resolutions she turned and saw me, and smiled.

'Hello, stranger,' she said. 'D'you want some tea? I boiled the kettle.'

'Thanks.' I got myself a mug, poured hot water on a tea bag and drew a deep breath.

'Mum, about these meetings of yours. What if I wanted to come in? Would they let me?'

'Oh Alan!' It was as if I'd spoken a magic word. She jumped down from her stool, eyes like stars. 'I'll e-mail Dittany, right now –'

'Hey, hey. Hold on! I said *what if*? But what if I did come along? What exactly happens?'

She stopped smiling and stared at me, biting her lip.

'Alan ... I don't know where to begin. It's *strange*. Almost scary.'

Then I had that *things coming together* feeling again, but much stronger. A shiver went up my spine.

Call it a premonition.

'It's not *strange*,' I said, automatically taking the sensible line. 'I refuse to believe there's anything *strange* about your latest load of old codswallop. It's the same old tricks, with a computer screen thrown in to make you feel you're getting something new. Go down to the pier, you can get a computer print-out of your horoscope. It's still a stupid horoscope. First they get people like you hooked with their jargon, and start letting you read their 'messages from the Beyond' on their Internet site. That's easy. It's like fortune-telling. They do a bit of research, ask a few questions, and they have plenty of information that they can whack into shape as authentic chat from a lost loved one. Then, in case the customers start realizing how easily those messages can be faked, they set up these 'meetings', where you can all get together and they can tell you how they've fixed some miraculous reunions –'

There were no stars in her eyes by now. She was looking angry.

'If that's how you feel, why do you suddenly want to come along?'

'I'm sorry. I didn't mean to get aggressive. I just hate to see you fooled, Mum.'

She calmed down. 'Well, okay. I can understand that. But it's nothing like what you imagine, Alan. The last two meetings, I was the only subscriber there. It was only for me.'

Again, I felt that shiver. Something dread, something strange –

I folded my arms. 'Go on then, tell me. What happens, while I'm waiting for you?'

'Alan, they have videos of her.'

So we were back to normal. The usual rubbish. I sighed, almost with relief. 'You mean, they've shown you a video of a girl who might be Stacey? That's nothing. Remember the time those people in Norway had us convinced they'd found her? They said their neighbours had adopted a little girl, and no one knew where she'd come from, and she looked exactly like those photos of Stacey on your webpage. You started imagining Stacey could have been carried off by a freak wave and hauled out of the sea by Norwegian fisher-folk . . . Then they sent us a tape they'd made. Their "Stacey" turned out to be a twelve-year-old with brown eyes and dark hair –'

Mum shook her head. 'I said "video", but that's the wrong word. It's not on a screen and there's no *background*, only the child. It's more like seeing a ghost.'

The word 'ghost' made me jump.

'You've seen Stacey's ghost?' I said it quickly, to prove I wasn't afraid of the word.

'Maybe . . . maybe the "ghost" of a living girl. That's what they say. Apparently, NIMROD technology captures her astral self from the spiritual plane, like the messages, downloads her into a computer system, and project these interviews – that's what you'll see, an interview with a living ghost – as they're happening, in real time. They say it's very rare to get such clear images. You won't believe it: it's as if she's there, alive and breathing in front of you. That's what makes Dittany sure that she's alive, wherever she is. The hunters still have to locate the child in the material world. But it might be Stacey, Alan. It really might.'

'I don't know what you're talking about, but I'm sure it's simply a cheap trick. They're playing you along, Mum. They're a bunch of crooks.'

'I know,' she sighed, taking me by surprise. She

laughed at my expression. 'You think I'm a gullible fool, Alan. But I'm not as daft as all that. I'm sure a lot of things about NIMROD are fake. I don't believe there ever was a Colonel Proctor of the US Armed Forces. And I've been asking around. None of my net-friends has heard of this huge global missing persons agency. You're right, they're chancers using modern technology to impress. *But that's not the whole story.* There's something going on here, different from any lead we've ever had before. Oh Alan, what do I care if they *are* crooks, if they can give Stacey back to us? And they want you to get involved, which is strange if they're complete crooks, isn't it? They know you're sceptical: you'd think they'd want to keep you away from their workings. But it's no use talking. You won't understand unless you see for yourself. Please, let me tell Dittany you're ready.'

My skin was creeping as if cold ants were crawling all over me.

'I said okay, didn't I? Fix it up.'

# Six

*M*Y MUM AND I WENT DOWN TO THE SEAFRONT together on a warm, hazy evening. The summer weather and the calm sea had to make us think about Stacey, but neither of us spoke about the day she had disappeared. We just went and gazed at the blue horizon for a few minutes, and then headed for the meeting that had been arranged, specially for me. The pub NIMROD used was called The Maypole. It was in a big Victorian block that was suffering from Developers' Blight. Soon the whole thing would be razed to the ground, and something new and bright and profitable would rise in its place. Meantime The Maypole was doing all right, but the upper floors were decrepit, with tiers of dirty windows, peeling paint and cracked plaster. We met Dittany in the saloon bar, where she was sitting alone but looking very much at home, with a glass and a cigarette. She offered to buy us a drink. Mum declined. Dittany said something cheery to the fat landlord, who was standing wiping a tankard and staring at us, and out we went around the back, where a dark little alley separated the block from the blank wall of some other building. We had to use a different door to get to the upstairs room. I stopped to glance down the alley.

'What's the matter?' asked Mum, who holding on to my arm as if she was afraid I'd change my mind and bolt. 'Are you all right, Alan?'

'I'm fine.'

There was plenty wrong, though nothing to do with

what I'd seen in the alley. But it was something I couldn't explain to my mum, no more than I'd been able to explain myself to Caz or Jo, when they told me I ought to 'go along' with NIMROD.

I was scared. I think I'd been scared since that afternoon when Dittany turned up at our house, and started talking about communicating with the spirits. Things that had happening since, like the connection with the sunbather, my lost witness, had persuaded me that there was a mystery that I had to investigate. But now that I was on the brink, my fear returned. It was different for Mum. She believed that Stacey was alive. No matter what Jo had hoped, it was obvious to me that NIMROD hadn't done anything to shake her certainty. But I had seen my sister's ghost. I knew such things were possible. And sometimes, Dittany had told us, NIMROD's messages came from the dead.

I knew the whole thing was a fake, of course it was a fake. *But suppose it wasn't?* There was a third child in me, a brainless kid of thirteen, who was afraid that NIMROD had really contacted Stacey's spirit. In a few minutes I would have to face my dead sister: and she would tell my mum that I had spent our bus fares. And more, oh much more than that: *what would I say to her?* What would I say – if she could speak and understand – to my lost little sister? What would I say if she asked me, *where's my life, Alan?*

This is the way I was thinking, as Dittany led the way into a dirty lobby and up a dusty, dirty flight of stairs. My skin was creeping, the air was cold and cloying. I looked up . . . and there was Stacey. Barefoot, blank-eyed, her sea-darkened hair straggling, she stood holding out her hands as if she was trying to bar the way.

'Alan? *Alan*, what is it?'

I realized Mum was shaking my arm, looking alarmed. The thing I could see was not visible to her. It was my private Stacey, not NIMROD's high-tech ghost. 'Nothing,' I said. 'Touch of indigestion. I'm okay.'

I had to walk through her. It was sickening: although I felt nothing and I'd closed my eyes.

Another door. Here we had to do those embarrassing handsigns. I tried to shuffle by. But the NIMROD doorman was as big as a nightclub bouncer, and he wasn't taking any chances. I had to satisfy him that I was one of the faithful.

We went into a big, gloomy hall. A few tables and chairs were standing about aimlessly. Scraps of streamers dangled from the walls, left over from some sad, long-ago Christmas party. In the middle of the floor a handful of chairs were arranged in a circle, under the dim lights that hung from the centre of the ceiling. There was a flash-looking PC set up, with a monitor and speakers, standing on a table. On either side of the table stood a pair of tall tripods, holding more equipment that I couldn't identify. Power cables snaked across the grimy boards. Apart from the main bouncer, who stayed by the door, there were three other big, hefty men dressed in black jeans and T-shirts. I supposed they were needed to hump the gear, but they were funny-looking customers to meet at a missing persons tea party. It made you wonder, did NIMROD meetings usually involve riot control? But there were hardly enough of us for a riot today. Apart from the big guys, me and my mum and Dittany, and one other man who was busy tapping away at the computer keyboard, the room was empty. Dittany went over to this man, and they started muttering together.

'Is this what it was like before?' I asked Mum, softly.

'The first two meetings were social. More what you'd imagine: other subscribers, people I didn't know who had also signed up with NIMROD. I was surprised that they were all strangers, I thought I knew most people in the area who were . . . like us. We chatted and had tea. The third time was like this. I think they were deciding if I could be trusted –'

'Trusted in what way – ?'

'Not to blab. They don't like publicity, Dittany told you that. It's a very strict rule.'

We fell silent, and waited respectfully until the man at the keyboard turned around and hopped to his left. He was not very tall, bulky rather than fat, and half-bald. Wisps of sandy hair curled behind his ears. He was wearing blue jeans and a polo shirt, casual wear that made him difficult to place. He could have been anything (when he wasn't fleecing trusting souls like Mum). A bus driver, a building worker, a businessman.

'Alan, this is Doric.'

Doric, she's told me, was the 'spirit name' of the boss. The computer whizz. He nodded at me briefly, after giving me a hard but not unfriendly stare.

'How d'you do, Alan. Has your mum told you what to expect?'

'Not really.'

'Good. I asked her not to prepare you. Sit over there.'

Mum and I sat down, Dittany between us. One of the spare bouncers went to join his friend by the door. Another of them stood by Doric, as if awaiting orders. The third came and sat down opposite me, and stared. I tried not to take it personally.

'Could we have some silence?' The boss had been working at his keyboard again. I'd kept an eye on the monitor screen, but I hadn't seen anything appear on it except lines of incomprehensible computer-program. No one was talking, but he raised his voice jovially, without looking round, while his fingers went on working: rattling, pausing, rattling on again.

'A bit of 'ush, while I do my Mystic-Meg routine, please.'

I wondered if we were supposed to chuckle, but decided against it.

Then he turned around, his arm casually along the back of the chair. For such an ordinary, not very attractive-looking little bloke, he had a lot of self assurance. 'Now. The interview is about to begin. A few house rules. This is mostly for your benefit, Alan, since you haven't been with us before. DO NOT address the apparition. Leave that to the channeller. KEEP SILENT while the apparition is present: don't talk among yourselves, and especially DO NOT distract the channeller. You can make notes, if a question occurs to you, and you can pass these notes to the channeller. She'll ask your question if she thinks it advisable, or deal with the topic in a later session if not. Her decision is final. Don't move out of your chairs, and above all DO NOT try to touch her. If you do, we might lose the connection for ever.'

He left the keyboard, moving lightly on the balls of his feet, and did some adjusting of the tripods. He must have given a sign for one of the bouncers by the door to switch off the lights, because the gloom suddenly became deeper. The computer monitor screen glowed blue and blank. I should have been paying more attention to what happened next. But it was so gloomy in there, and I was thinking of the ghost that I'd seen on the stairs. I was hoping my mum couldn't see how I was trembling, I was praying that nothing too weird would happen, because I didn't think I could stand it . . .

Suddenly, a child was there.

She had a yellowish-brown hair in a ponytail, a freckled nose and a dimple in her round chin. She was wearing a blue tracksuit with a pink trim, and trainers. The clothes weren't new, they looked well-worn. She was three-dimensional but slightly transparent, like a hologram. I tried moving my head. She didn't vanish if you changed your viewpoint.

'Stacey?' came Dittany's hoarse croak. 'Can you hear us?'

'Yes,' said the little girl, looking round as if puzzled. 'But I can't see you.'

'Where are you?'

'I'm in the grey place,' said the girl. 'I *think* I'm dreaming,' she added, with a frown.

We mustn't speak, but I almost cried out. The voice was different. This girl was older, the face had changed, but *that was Stacey's funny little frown* –

'Tell us something about yourself.'

'My favourite book is called *The Little Red Hen*,' said the image. She began to skip from foot to foot. 'I like tomatoes, I like cheese, I like biting Alan's knees. Where's Torquil?'

'Who is Torquil?'

'Well, he's a dinosaur *now*. But he used to be a duck.'

'Where are you, Stacey?'

'I'm in the grey place.'

'When you're not dreaming, where are you?'

'Still in the grey place, where they keep me. Can you let me out?'

It went on. Dittany asked questions and the child answered. Some of the questions she read from a sheet of paper. I saw my mum nodding, and I guessed these were questions that she had devised. After a few minutes, 'Stacey's' expression changed. Her lip trembled, her eyes went wide: it was as if for the first time she could see us, the strange room, the strangers staring at her.

'Mummy!' she cried. 'Mummy? Oh dear, oh dear . . .'

I heard my mum catch her breath. *Oh dear, oh dear*: that was what Stacey would say if she was scared or hurting.

'She's waking,' croaked Dittany.

And the image was gone.

The voice stayed a moment longer. We heard it whimper away into silence –

*'Mummy, I had a bad dream!'*

The lights went on again.

'Blast it,' growled Doric. He had been standing by one of the tripods, in the shadows. 'Why can't you channellers ask them straight questions?'

He slipped something into his pocket: a palm-sized, smoothly dimpled object, like a fancy remote control.

'I'm doing my best,' croaked Dittany. 'Can't push it. She's a child, that makes it more difficult. The child's asleep and dreaming, the harder you question her the sooner she wakes.'

'So, think of some *softly, softly – gently, gently* way to ask her where she lives!' Doric turned away impatiently. 'Mrs Robarts, could I have a word?'

He led my mum away from the dim lights, and talked to her in a heated whisper. I couldn't hear what he was saying, but Mum was nodding a lot.

We left soon after. One of the bouncer blokes let us out. Dittany came with us to the street, and then went back upstairs.

'I think I'll call a taxi,' said Mum. 'You're as white as a sheet, Alan.'

She went to call the taxi from the bar of The Maypole. I said I preferred to stay out in the fresh air. As soon as she was gone, I took a few steps down that side alley. The red car was still there. The same red car that I had seen before, once near to this pub, once in a street near that house in the suburbs, and once beside the restaurant by the station. I was certain it was the same car, though I hadn't noticed the numberplates the first two times. The windows were heavily tinted, but I could see someone in the driver's seat.

Mum came back and found me standing on the corner. 'It'll be here in a few minutes. Well? What do you think now?'

'I can't think, not yet . . .'

She nodded. 'I understand. I know I felt knocked out after my first time.'

'Would you mind if I walked home? I mean, by myself.'

She took my hand and squeezed it. 'You need to be alone. We'll talk later.'

The taxi arrived. Mum got into the back and it drove away. I went down the alley. I walked up to the red car and rapped on the dark glass of the driver's window.

It could have been one of the NIMROD people, it could have been just anyone . . .

She wound the window down and looked out at me. My hunch had been right.

She was bareheaded this time. Her hair was short and blonde. She wasn't smiling. But without the smile, without the ammonite earrings, the baseball cap or the sunglasses, I still recognized her at once. 'So,' she said. 'What happened, Alan?' Why didn't you keep our appointment?'

'Better late than never.'

She leaned over and opened the passenger door for me. I went round and climbed in.

'Okay,' I said, trying to sound as if I was in charge. 'Start explaining.'

'Let's get away from here first. Would you like a drink? I'll take you to Jonno's.'

'Jonno's' wasn't far. We left the red car in the car park. She seemed to be a regular. The woman behind the bar, a thin slinky girl with a silver ring in her nose and another in her eyebrow, said 'Hi'. She ordered a whisky sour. I asked for a Coke. We took our drinks to a booth. It was a long, low, shadowy room. A few other customers were scattered about, but the place was very quiet – except for the muted soundtrack from an alcove where some arcade games were playing their trailers.

'You know my name,' I said. 'I don't know yours.'

'You can call me Demetria.'

Another 'D'.

'So you are one of these NIMROD people?'

'Not exactly. You're right though, it's not my real name. Will it do for now?'

'I don't care what you call yourself. Just tell me what's going on.'

She sipped her drink. She had a neat figure, lean and sporty, in a tight-fitting white T-shirt. Her face was a smooth, tanned oval, wide across the eyes and narrowing to a pointed chin. Her eyes were a cool, tawny grey. I looked her over frankly, and this time I was totally sure. 'It *was* you, that day. When you came into Countryfare I thought you were messing around. I thought you might be a journalist who'd read my story and dressed up as the lost witness to get me to talk for some creepy *where are they now* feature. But it *was* you.'

'Yes, it was me.'

'Why didn't you come forward?'

I asked the easy question first. And I asked it quietly. It was too late to shout and yell.

'I'm sorry, Alan, but I couldn't. I'll explain why not . . . soon. In any case, at the time I didn't know you needed me. It wasn't until long afterwards that I realized I'd been one of the last people to see the little girl who disappeared –'

I felt my face go red. 'Yes. That was my fault. I told a stupid lie, at first.'

'And by then my story wouldn't have changed anything, so –'

I swallowed hard. 'But you saw. You must have s-seen what happened.'

She shook her head. 'I'm sorry, Alan.'

'*What do you mean?*'

'I mean, I didn't see. I mean, I don't know what happened to your sister.'

I couldn't take this in.

'But that's not possible. You *must* have seen . . . You were right there. What happened to you? Where did you vanish to? Didn't you see me searching for her?'

She winced and grimaced, pain and sympathy in her grey eyes. 'I knew this would be bad,' she said. 'Look,

—— 51 ——

Alan, I can't tell you much, not yet. You're going to have to trust me, because I need your help and you need mine. I *didn't* see you searching. I think I must have left the spot where you met me before you were out of sight the first time. I was looking for something myself, that day: something very important.'

I stared at her, but what I saw was the sea defences, grey knucklebones under the white face of the cliff; a bright blue sky. I was scrambling up and down, shouting frantically: 'Stacey! Stacey!' But where was my sunbather? Was there a towel still spread on the stones? Was it possible that she was anywhere near that place, and didn't hear me yelling?

'You didn't see her fall? You didn't see me come back?'

'Alan, listen to me. I swear I did not see your sister fall. Like I said: it must have been just after I spoke to you two, after I told you about the cliff path, that I got up and left. I didn't see either of you again.'

I couldn't believe it. My witness was here, and *still* I didn't know the truth.

'So how can you help me, if you didn't see what happened?'

'Don't you want to get your sister back?'

For a moment I was too stunned to speak. She took a sip of whisky.

'My sister is dead,' I said flatly.

'Are you sure about that? Alan, I know what you saw up there, upstairs at The Maypole. I know what NIMROD will have shown you –'

'That's why you turned up again, isn't it? You know something about NIMROD. You knew that weird woman Dittany was going to approach my mother. This is all tied together.'

'Somehow,' she agreed. 'So, do you want to get your sister back?'

'You're talking nonsense. She's dead. That stuff about

locating her on the astral plane is pure gibberish. It's a con-trick.'

But I felt like a hypnotized rabbit. *I like tomatoes, I like cheese, I like biting Alan's knees.* How could NIMROD have found out about that? A silly rhyme I made up for my sister when she was three years old, long before she disappeared. And there'd been other details, things I was sure Mum hadn't told them, things that couldn't have been recorded in the newspaper archives or anywhere else. How could they train a kid to wrinkle up her nose and poke herself in the eye: the weird contortions only Stacey could have invented, to help her to concentrate. *I think I'm dreaming . . .*

I tried to lift my glass, but that was a mistake because my hand was shaking. I nearly spilled Coke all over the table. When it strikes you out of the blue, when you are totally unprepared, hope can be as terrifying as fear.

'I don't understand!'

'I know. And I can't explain, not yet. Alan, if you are sure, completely, absolutely sure, that your sister is dead, get up and walk away. You have nothing to lose.'

We waited, each of us staring at the other. I stayed in my chair. It was as if three years hadn't happened. She was smiling at me with the sun behind her, telling me she could save my life . . .

'All right. What do you want me to do?'

Demetria sighed – with relief, I thought. 'For the moment, nothing. Go to another session. Make up your mind whether that could be your sister. Keep your eyes and ears open. I'll be in touch. Don't follow me now. Wait a few minutes before you leave.'

She stood up, and walked out of the bar.

# Seven

THE NEXT MEETING WAS AT THE PLACE OUT IN THE suburbs again. We arrived at the front door, and Dittany let us in. She hadn't paid much attention to me at The Maypole, or maybe I'd been too scared to notice. She made a fuss of me this time, telling me how glad she was I'd overcome my prejudice, and how much it meant to my mum to have me involved. But I had a feeling those hooded eyes were watching me closely. I tried to act as if I'd become a believer.

The front hall was nicely furnished, but strangely chill on that warm evening. The room she took us into seemed to have been cleared of furniture for NIMROD's benefit. There was a carpet on the floor and curtains at the windows, but none of the armchairs, sofa and TV sort of things you'd expect in someone's living room. I even saw marks on the walls where pictures had been taken down.

It was the same as the set-up in the room above The Maypole: the computer, the tripod things, the bouncers and Doric. The whole atmosphere was so different from what I'd imagined when I left Mum at the door here, last time. Instead of a bunch of nice, helpless people getting together over tea and biscuits to share their troubles, there was this stripped-down, serious, experimental apparatus: the big ominous-looking men, the busy-fingered, self-confident computer whizz. The feeling that something exciting and important was going on was impressive, I had to admit. The lights were dimmed, the curtains closed. Doric did his routine of chatting breezily while he tapped keys and fixed the tripods.

And we saw the kid who was supposed to be Stacey again.

She was wearing the same faded tracksuit, her feet were bare. Her hair was loose and tousled this time. She sat cross-legged, not quite on the same level as the carpet but hovering above it. As before, Mum and I had to keep silent while Dittany asked the questions. As before, she claimed she could hear Dittany, but couldn't see or hear any of the rest of us.

Dittany, presumably under orders from the boss, had given up the softly-softly approach, and kept asking direct questions. It didn't do any good. When she was asked *where are you?* 'Stacey' would answer either *I'm dreaming*, or *I'm in the grey place*. When Dittany asked where she lived when she was awake, and tried to get her to describe her house and garden or where she went to school, she didn't seem to understand.

She was more skittish this time. She wanted to show us how she could pull on her big toes when she was sitting with her legs crossed, and make them both touch her belly – one of *our* Stacey's favourite tricks. She got up and started skipping about, as if she was bored.

Dittany asked, *who looks after you?*

The little girl wrinkled up her nose, stuck a finger on either side of it as if she was trying to squeeze out her eyeballs, and said firmly, 'I don't think she is my mummy.'

'Why do you say that?'

'Because it's what I *think*!' said 'Stacey' impatiently. 'My mummy and my daddy and my Alan are all not here. I'm lost. I'm far from home. When I'm awake I forget that, but when I'm asleep, I remember.'

Mum and I were sitting with Dittany between us – not our idea, that was the way we'd been arranged. I heard Mum stirring impatiently. *'Ask her,'* she begged, in a whisper (against the rules, we were supposed to keep silent). 'Ask when did she last see her real mummy. Ask her what happened. See if she remembers that day –'

The room wasn't very dark. I could see Dittany purse her lipsticked mouth. She shook her head in warning. 'That'll wake her,' she warned. The little girl stood looking round, apparently puzzled by the silence of this voice that asked her questions in her dreams. I could see the wall of the room through her face.

'Do you remember when you last saw your own mummy?'

'Not when I'm awake,' said the child.

'But you're dreaming now, Stacey.'

She started to hop up and down violently, the tousled hair flying. Watch out, I thought, knowing the signs. Stace was heading for a tantrum.

'Hepup! Hepup! I'm captured in a Chinese fortune factory!'

'Losing the signal –' reported Doric from his place at the keyboard.

The image began to flicker. The little girl's wilful, stubborn little face dissolved –

'Stacey!' said Dittany, sharply. 'Stacey, *don't* wake up –'

But she was gone.

The session had lasted for longer this time. When Doric's bouncers switched on the lights my head was swimming. I hadn't realized it, but I'd been concentrating furiously. Mum was in a worse state. As soon as the lights went up she slumped forward in her chair, face buried in her hands. Dittany put an arm round her shoulders.

'Let me get you a drink of water, love.'

'No. Thank you, but I'm all right.'

Doric shut the computer down and flicked some switches on the stands of the tripod things. He came over. 'Mrs Robarts,' he began, 'I know how hard this is –'

Mum looked up, wiping her eyes with her fingers.

'Where is she?' she demanded. 'You've got to tell me. Wherever that little girl is, I *have to see her.* I have to touch her, I have to talk to her myself. How else can I be sure?'

'Well, we're narrowing it down,' said Doric blandly. 'From the strength of the signal we're convinced she's in Europe. From the speech-recognition analysis, we know she doesn't speak English, French or Italian as her waking language. We could be looking at Germany, we could be looking at somewhere farther east.'

'My God. How long is this going to go on?'

'Mrs Robarts, you have to be patient. We're dealing with a child. This is the first time we've used the NIMROD technique on such a young subject. We can't ask her the questions we can ask an adult, without distressing her so much that we lose contact. You've seen that for yourself. Frankly, I'm thrilled with our results.' His tone was reproachful. 'I'm surprised that you're not thrilled yourself. We're picking up emissions from a displaced child's dreaming brain, and condensing them digitally into a moving, speaking image. I'm a computer scientist, Mrs Robarts. I leave the spiritual plane to others in this organization. As far as I'm concerned everything we do has a rational basis in the laws of physics. But isn't what we've done for you so far miraculous enough? Trust us. I think we'll soon have her precise location.'

Mum's expression, as she listened to the NIMROD boss, was such a mixture of distrust and longing, I didn't know if she was going to hit him or fall down and kiss his feet. She reached out a hand to me (I was standing by her side, not sure what to do with myself), and clutched my arm.

'I'm sure of one thing,' she said. 'It's time to tell her father. I can't keep Matt out any longer. He has to see this for himself.'

Matt was my dad. Knowing how he felt about the Stacey Search, I didn't think trying to bring him in on this was a good idea. But I was surprised to find that Doric agreed with me, after the trouble he and Dittany had taken to get *me* involved. His reassuring expression changed in a flash. 'Oh no,' he said. 'You mustn't do that, Mrs Robarts.' Dittany, who'd come back with a glass of water, had also heard. She was behind Doric, pulling faces to warn Mum she'd gone too far.

'No publicity,' she croaked. 'It's in the contract you signed, you know.'

Doric became grave and stern. 'Mrs Robarts, I must *insist* that you don't contact your ex-husband. If you do that . . . It would be very, very sad. But if you or your son reveal details of these advanced techniques to anyone outside NIMROD, I'd have to think seriously about continuing with the search, much as I'd regret letting you down. Do you understand?'

'I understand,' said Mum quickly. The threat was veiled: dressed up in kind, concerned smiles. But he was telling her that if she didn't behave, he would take her baby away again. 'I won't say anything. I agreed to your conditions, and I'll keep to them. I was thinking of being fair to Matt –'

Doric patted her on the shoulder. My mum's tall, like me. He had to reach up.

'That's a good girl. Wait until you can tell him the best good news of his life. Don't *worry*, Mrs Robarts. Believe me, things are going very, very well indeed. Soon, very soon, you'll have the result you hardly dared to dream of.'

The NIMROD people wanted to call us a taxi, but we decided to walk back to the bus stop. We left them in that silent house, and didn't speak until we'd put a couple of streets of well-heeled greenery and flowerbeds behind us. It was a part of town that neither of us knew.

'It's an empty house, isn't it?' said Mum at last. 'They use it without the owners knowing.'

'I thought that. I wonder how they happen to have the key.'

'Maybe Doric is an estate agent, when he's not being NIMROD's computer scientist.'

She started to laugh, but there were tears in her eyes. 'Oh Alan, I think I'm going to go mad. It's Stacey. It *is* Stacey, isn't it? You think so too.'

'It can't be,' I protested. 'Honestly, Mum, it *can't be*.'

'You say that. But I saw how you reacted when she was there. You *feel* that it's Stacey. Older, different: maybe not what we expected. But it's her.'

Our whole lives had been turned upside down. The NIMROD business had started as another futile exercise, another way to keep Mum going from day to day. Now everything was up for grabs. I could smell the warm tar from the road surface, melted by the day's hot sun; it was mingled with the scent of roses. Summer smells – bringing back that other summer, when my misery had been fresh and new.

'Look, Mum, all I know is that Doric's "scientific" explanation has to be hogwash. That stuff about "losing the signal" and "condensing an image from dream-emissions". I know computer science is a wonderful thing and you can digitize anything these days. I know you can get machines that pick up people's brain waves. But I'm sure there's no such technology.'

Mum shrugged. 'You mean there wasn't, until now. You can't tell. For all we know that man Doric is a genius, testing out a fantastic new invention.'

'I thought you said they were crooks.'

She shook her head impatiently. 'Oh Alan, what does it matter? Crooks, or an eccentric scientist and his team. I told you before, when we were at The Maypole. *I don't care*. I don't care how or why they do what they do. They've found her, she's alive. That's the important thing. I don't care how many lies they tell me, or how much I have to bow and scrape and do what I'm told. *I want Stacey*. They have contact with her. That's what matters.'

I gave up. I wasn't going to get through to her. My mum had years of practice at believing things other people couldn't believe in.

'So you're not going to tell Dad?'

'Not Dad, or anyone. I can't risk losing her.'

I'd guessed why Doric was so determined to keep my dad out of it. They'd done their research. I was harmless, but they probably knew how Dad, my dad, would react to this kind of show . . . He wouldn't keep any vows of secrecy! Maybe I should tell him myself. But I couldn't do that. I imagined the hell there would be, between him and Mum, if he tried to make her give up on these people who had actually shown her Stacey, alive . . . I could have laughed, bitterly, at the way NIMROD had us tied up in knots. So much for Jo Brennan's hopes. We were in NIMROD's power all right, no question of that. We'd reached the bus stop. I looked up the road. There was a bus coming.

'Mum, I –'

She gave me a watery smile. 'I know, don't tell me. You want to be alone, you want to think.' She hugged me. 'Oh, Alan, my big little boy. If nothing else, it's *good* to have you back. Don't try to walk all the way home. It's miles.'

I watched her get on the bus, and then headed off the way we'd come. Those suburban Drives and Closes were so alike you could easily get lost, but my main worry was that the NIMROD team would be hanging around. However, I didn't see them. I found Demetria's red car near where I'd seen it before, discreetly parked in a cul-de-sac. She'd seen me coming. She opened the door and I climbed in.

'We meet again,' she said, with a wry smile. 'Well? What do you think now?'

Without waiting for an answer she began to drive. It was a nice car. Small but expensive, inside and out. I felt the chill of the air-conditioning. Whatever kind of secret agent she was, she wasn't short of money.

I stared through the tinted windscreen, trying to think clearly (which was difficult around Mum, who coloured everything with her desperate hope). I decided I had to stop wondering how they did the 'living ghost', and concentrate on the child herself. It *couldn't* be Stacey, I knew that. But Mum was right, I had nearly fallen under the spell . . . Why? What made this little girl so convincing? Stacey had been tall for her age. I thought the girl we saw, if she was eight, was smaller than average, if anything. And thin, while Stacey had been a chunky kid. Her eyes were like Stacey's eyes: the same pale blue, the same bold look, the same stubby dark lashes and arched brows. Her chin had that cleft, in the right place. There was something about her *smile* that was different. Maybe it was the teeth, the two big front teeth, instead of Stacey's little pearlie-whites.

She sometimes didn't talk like an eight-year-old. *My mummy and my daddy and my Alan are all not here . . .* She'd said that like a little child. But then, she was dreaming. She could be reverting to the age she'd been when she had last spoken English in the waking world. It made sense. Yes, even the rough edges made sense.

*Hepup! Hepup! I'm captured in a Chinese fortune factory –*

The Christmas before she vanished, after the turkey and so on, we pulled our crackers and read out the jokes. I told that old joke about the Chinese fortune cookie. Someone opens up the piece of paper from inside the cookie, and instead of telling his fortune, the message says: *help, I'm being held prisoner in a Chinese Fortune Cookie Factory*. Stacey didn't get it, naturally. She had no idea what a Chinese Fortune Cookie was. That didn't stop her laughing her face off. It was a minor moment in an uneasy Christmas truce (this was soon after my parents had separated. Having Dad back for the festivities had been strained). I remembered it because Stacey had been so delighted with her version of the punch line. For ages afterward she loved to chant it, and roared with laughter every time.

How did NIMROD know about that? How did they know that my little sister, from when she first learned to talk, used to say *hepup*, when she meant 'help'?

And I knew this was impossible, even according to the NIMROD version, but I was sure that the little girl I'd just seen had been *talking to no one but me*, when she cried for help.

This was no good. The more I tried to talk myself out of it, the more confused I felt –

'Have you fallen asleep? Or are you going to tell me if you think that's Stacey?'

I had to fight against the cruel temptation she offered me. I *couldn't* let myself hope. 'I don't know what's going on. I don't know what to make of it at all. But that's not my sister.'

'How can you be so sure?' asked Demetria, keeping her eyes on the road.

'Because it can't be. Because my sister's dead.'

'You say that as if you have proof.'

I wondered what she'd think if I told her it was *Stacey herself* who had warned me not to trust NIMROD. I closed my eyes. I could see again that figure standing on the stairs at The Maypole, holding out her hands to bar the way. A solid little ghost, not transparent like the 'living' Stacey I'd just watched jumping about in someone's deserted living room. Stacey, the way I had seen her the day she died, the day the life I used to have ended. Now here I was driving along in a fast car, with a beautiful stranger who seemed to be trying to draw me into a mysterious, exciting adventure. The situation was so bizarre, I was hardly surprised to hear myself confessing the secret I had told to no one else.

'I see her ghost,' I said. 'I've been seeing her off and on, since a few weeks after . . . you know. I see her around our house, looking the way she did the day she vanished. Still wet from the sea. She doesn't speak, she doesn't do anything. But she's never going to leave me alone. I've never told anyone before, but it's the truth. How can I doubt that she's dead, when her ghost is haunting me?'

The car drew to a halt. I'd been staring through the windscreen without seeing anything outside it. Now I recognized where she'd brought me, and it was inevitable. We were on the cliffs, in the car park at the beginning of the clifftop path to Seastead. The evening sky was wide and beautiful. Behind us the sun had dipped below the horizon, but the sea still glittered softly in the afterglow. Demetria looked at me with sympathy.

'You think it was all your fault, don't you?'

'If you know what happened . . . and I'm sure you do. You seem to know everything. You know it *was* my fault.'

'You blame yourself too much. You didn't do anything terrible, you simply had very bad luck. That's the way I read it. I believe you, when you say you've seen her ghost. But that doesn't mean she's dead, Alan. It could be something that happens because you feel so guilty. What you see is real to you, but it's in your mind. It has nothing to do with Stacey herself.'

'It's all in my mind?' I shrugged. 'What if it is? What's the difference? I think that's where "haunting" happens, in real life. In people's minds. Ghosts are guilt and grief, and fear, that our minds give the form of monsters; or of the people we've harmed. They take shape from what you're feeling. I see my sister's ghost because I know she's dead. I know she's dead because there's no other possible explanation.'

Demetria was playing with her sunglasses, opening and shutting the ear pieces as she held them on her lap. 'Sounds as if you've done a lot of thinking about things, Alan.'

'I've had a lot of time for it.' Too much, I thought.

She looked up, and studied my face, seriously. 'Mr

Shelf-filler Alan,' she said. 'Thinking his life away. You're an interesting person, did you know that? Then she put the glasses aside, and turned her back on me, quickly, as if she was afraid she was giving too much away.

'Come on. I want to show you something.'

I hadn't been back here. The vivid memories I had of this scene, this exact scene in burning daylight, were those of a thirteen-year-old kid. I'd dreamed about the clifftop path, night after night: horrible dreams of running, running till my heart burst and still failing to reach somewhere in time. But the waking had been worse.

In real life everything looked strangely harmless. We walked on the springy turf. There was a light breeze from the sea, and a salt tang in the air.

'I work for an investigation bureau,' said Demetria. 'Three years ago I was down there on the sea defences because I was looking for some crucial evidence. I think your sister vanished because she found what I was looking for. In those few minutes when she was alone, she saw something that she could not be allowed to tell. So she was snatched away.' She paused, looking out to sea. 'They didn't kill her. Let's give them the benefit of the doubt, and say they didn't kill her because she was only a little girl, and they had no reason to wish her dead. Instead they took her away. Maybe they took her to another country, and found her a new home. But they kept an eye on her. So when they needed her, they could fetch her back.'

'I don't get it, Demetria.' I supposed I might as well call her by the only name I knew. 'Say Stacey was kidnapped, in some weird miraculous way, from halfway up these cliffs, and made to vanish for three years. Say these NIMROD people were the kidnappers. Then what made them suddenly decide to contact us again? Why now? That's the real question ... I mean it would be, if I believed any of this.'

'I'm not sure.' She frowned, speaking hesitantly as if

she was feeling her way. 'But I can guess, and it's tied up with the mystery I was investigating. I think something has happened that makes Stacey a valuable hostage, and that's why they've brought her back into the game. I think the NIMROD people are trying to use your sister to get power over someone who could blow the cover on the whole thing.'

'What do you mean, the whole thing? What *is* "the whole thing"?'

She shook her head. 'If I told you all I know, you wouldn't believe me . . . I can only assure you, the people I work for aren't kooks, and they take this seriously.'

'Who *do* you work for, exactly? You make it sound like some kind of secret service.'

'I don't work for the government, if that's what you mean. It's a private company. But don't worry, we're on the side of law and order.' She looked frustrated. 'Alan, it's like this. Three years ago, I reached a dead end. Now I'm back on the track. I'm convinced NIMROD is the key to something very big. I'm convinced they are involved in the strange events I was investigating three years ago. I've been trying to find out what goes on inside this so-called missing persons recovery service. I managed to infiltrate them, which is how I got my "spirit name". But I need your help.'

'Let me get this straight. You're suggesting that they really do have my sister, alive.'

Demetria nodded, half smiling.

'Then why those – those hologram videos, or whatever you call them? Why don't they produce her, or have her talk on the phone, or something?'

'Isn't it obvious? As soon as they admit they're holding the child themselves, they're not high-tech missing persons finders any more. They're revealed as plain kidnappers. That's why you see Stacey's "living ghost", and you aren't allowed any contact with the child herself –'

'How do they *do* that stuff, anyway? I've never seen anything like it.'

'NIMROD can do a lot of strange things, Alan.'

'All adding up to some huge conspiracy you can't possibly explain.' I shook my head. 'No. I'm sorry, but no. As far as your conspiracy goes, you could be making it up or it could be true, I don't really care. But it must be some other kid that looks like her. That's not my sister.'

My sister was the dead little girl, who haunted my nights and days.

'Then how do they know, Alan? How do they know all those *little* things, the things you're sure you and your family never told the police, or anyone?'

It was strange the way she seemed to know everything that was going on in my mind. I looked at her doubtfully: I couldn't think of an answer. I shrugged.

She gazed around at the empty clifftop, sea and sky. The hum of traffic from the road mingled with the endless murmur of the waves, far below. 'Maybe I can change your mind. I said I wanted to show you something. But it's not here. If we arrange another meeting, will you turn up this time?'

'Yeah. I'll go along with you that far.'

'Good. Let's get back to town. On the way, I'll tell you what I want you to do.'

# Eight

$T$WO NIGHTS LATER I WAS DOWN ON BEACHCOMBE Marina, lurking outside the gates of the luxury housing compound that overlooks the yacht basin. It was ten o'clock at night, and this time I really *was* a burglar, hanging around with criminal intent. A small white van drew up beside me, in the dark between the pools of security lighting. It had a blue stripe along the body and a blurred sticker in the windscreen. The driver's door opened a crack.

'Hi,' said Demetria. 'Hop in. We'll change in the van.'

She was dressed in baggy dark blue overalls. She'd brought along the same for me and she had on some kind of face-makeup that gave her skin a grainy, stubbled and creased look: nothing heavy, but it really changed her. My overalls were the right size for my long legs. Over these suits we put yellow bibs with reflecting stripes, on our heads we wore peaked caps. No badges or anything, just a generally official-looking look. 'Nothing disguises you like a uniform,' she told me, grinning.

Each of us had a toolbag, to complete the effect. Mine was quite heavy.

Then things got really illegal. Demetria produced a little black plastic box, and pressed one end of it against the electronic lock on the gates. The lock buzzed and clicked, she pushed gently and the gates came open. We got into the lobby the same way. My heart leaped into my mouth when I saw a security guard there, behind a desk. But Demetria was relaxed. She ambled over, imitating perfectly the walk of a shambling little old tradesman, and mumbled something. The guard pushed across the visitors' register, and waited without showing the slightest interest while she made some kind of entry.

We took the lift to the top floor. The lights seemed very bright, and the security camera in the ceiling seemed to be staring straight at me. I kept my head down. Nobody was about. Demetria led the way along a smartly furnished hallway, with windows that looked over a magnificent sea view. She used her gadget at the front door of one of the flats (it had the kind of lock that opens with a keycard and a combination number). I followed her inside and waited, in fear and dread and excitement, while she disappeared into the gloom. After what seemed a long time – probably a couple of minutes – she came back, without her toolbag. She gave me a thumbs-up sign and a big grin, and flipped a few switches on the wall.

At once, all the lights came on. The room we were standing in was huge. It was decorated in grey and black and white, in the most classy taste, if you like the modern minimalist look. The only touches of colour were in the pictures on the walls, which were modern too: and you could tell they were expensive. The one I liked best was a big square thing, in a plain metal frame, that was simply a grid of grey dots on a white ground, but over this grid was scattered a handful of blood-red petals . . .

'Nice, isn't it?' said Demetria, in her normal voice.

'Wow!'

She giggled. 'It's like a film set, isn't it. Like a James Bond movie. And all computer-controlled for perfect service . . .' She saw that I was staring at the big square windows opposite us, which were uncovered and black as coal. This penthouse must be blazing like a beacon, if you were down in the car park or something – 'It's okay, that's reversible glass. Completely lightproof at the touch of a switch. One of the fancy tricks we'd like fully explained, by the way, along with their movie-making equipment.

The doors are light-sealed too. No one outside can tell that we're in here, and I've disabled the surveillance. Here, put these on before you touch anything.' She tossed me a packet that contained a pair of slick plastic gloves.

I laughed in amazement. I was thinking, as I put them on, *this cannot be me!* For a few minutes then, we were like two little kids in a playroom. Of course Demetria had been here before, and I guess *she* didn't forget for a moment that we were in the lair of a dangerous adversary. But I felt there was something in her that loved danger for its own sake; and she wakened the same nature in me. Something I'd forgotten for a long time, something wild.

There was a bedroom, a kitchen, a room that looked like a fully operational multimedia studio, another bedroom, a games room with a snooker table: all looking strangely unreal in the brilliant white light that we couldn't escape . . . I was peering into the bathroom when Demetria caught up with me. Beside the bath, which was round and sunk in the floor, there was a towel rack heaped with huge, fat, white fluffy towels; and a set of controls that looked like the instrumentation for a spaceship.

'Do you want to take a bath?' She laughed, but then she got serious. 'Time's up, Alan. We have to do the business now and get out. Or we're going to get caught.'

She led me into the studio, the place with all the media equipment in it.

'I'm going to show you a movie,' she said. I walked around, looking at things, while she flipped switches and moved toggles on a kind of mixing desk at the back of the room. There was a silver ashtray lying on one of these side desks, with the words *Diamond Life* stamped on the rim and outlined in tiny jewels. Yeah, I thought. That's this place all right. The diamond life . . .

In one of the drawers I opened there were cases full of small discs, like CD-ROM discs, but oval and matt black. I read the labels: but they were nothing but strings of numbers. In another I found a sleek, dimpled, greyish gizmo that I thought I recognized. Until that moment I'd half forgotten we were here to investigate NIMROD. Truth was, I hadn't taken much notice of anything Demetria said about the big conspiracy. I was simply fascinated and mystified: willing to go along with her for the ride, willing to take a few risks. I touched the thing – and got a shock. It seemed to be warm, like something alive. It seemed to mould itself into my hand.

I jerked my fingers away. They were tingling as if I'd touched a live wire.

'Yeah,' said Demetria. She'd been watching, over her shoulder. 'Some of their toys are very strange.' She turned back to her fiddling with the controls, with a secretive smile. 'Sit down, we're ready.'

I sat in one of the soft, deep chairs that were circled around a black table that took up most of the centre of the room. I didn't hear anything, but I could *feel* a faint humming. Something started to happen in the air above the middle of the table. An image took shape. I had no expectations, Demetria hadn't told me anything. I watched, as an ordinary tabby-and-white cat appeared – life-sized and three-dimensional but transparent, like the kid who was supposed to be Stacey. But this was an improvement on the living-ghost effect. In a second or two the transparency was gone. It was a *real* cat. I mean, completely real, so you couldn't believe it wasn't standing there. It walked about a bit, and then sat, upright, with its tail wrapped around its toes.

A pair of gloved human hands appeared. The rest of the person was a blur, but the hands and wrists were very real. They stroked the cat. It responded, putting up its tail and lifting its chin to be scratched. One of the hands vanished and reappeared: it was now holding a metal band, which was quickly wrapped around the cat's head. The cat took a moment to realize its trust had been betrayed, then it started to struggle and use its paws. It couldn't get rid of the band. It struggled frantically, teeth bared and eyes wild in panic.

The next part was sickening, but I couldn't look away. The cat's eyes bulged, its mouth gaped in a silent scream. There began to be blood trickling over the shiny metal that was wrapped around its head: the band was being tightened violently, by some means I couldn't see. The torture went on until, well, the cat's head broke; like a can squeezed in a fist. Its face was a red ruin, its fur spattered with grey brain tissue, blood and bone. The body flopped. The muscles jerked, and it lay still.

'That's disgusting –' I cried.

'Ssh. Watch.'

The hands came back – I hadn't noticed them disappear – and took away the metal strip. The dead cat started to move again. It staggered to its feet, the head still shattered. Over about ten seconds, the pieces came back together. The cat was alive again: but it didn't look happy. It cowered, visibly shaking, in the puddle of mess of its own blood and tissue.

'Well?' said Demetria. 'What do you think? Does that convince you?'

I was shaken, but not too impressed. 'You're trying to tell me they can kill a cat and bring it back to life? Don't make me laugh. You can't prove anything with special effects.'

She frowned. 'Forget the subject. That was just a random sample. I'm trying to tell you the images you've seen of your sister were created by the equipment in this studio.'

Actually, I didn't feel like laughing. It wasn't so much the futuristic technology that impressed me. Hologram movie-making equipment might not be in the shops yet, but it made more sense than 'condensed dream emissions'. But what I'd seen was horrible. I couldn't shrug it off: and I'd suddenly realized that there was a living child being used to make those NIMROD movies. It didn't matter if she was my sister or not. Suppose the NIM-ROD people decided to give her something like the treatment they'd given the cat –

Demetria was gazing at me fiercely, hopefully. I could see in her eyes that she was sick to death of trying to convince people of the reality of this threat, conspiracy, whatever it was –

She leaned forward, about to tell me something more. Over her shoulder, the cat was still there; cowering in misery. At that moment we both heard something. A small, ominous click, from somewhere in the other rooms.

Demetria gasped. 'Stay here!' she breathed, and moved swiftly and silently to the door. Of course I followed her. There was thick, soft carpet everywhere in that flat. We were able to sneak without a sound down the passage, to where we could see into the big room. Three bulky dark-clad figures had just entered and stood looking suspiciously around. With them was a smaller man. It was Doric, the computer whizz, NIMROD's eccentric inventor. But he looked very different from the bouncy, moody little man Mum and I had met. It wasn't only that he was more smartly dressed. It was as if everything about him now *explained* the self-assurance that had puzzled me. He looked as if he belonged in this expensive setting. He was rich, he was important, and definitely in charge –

They'd come home and found all the lights on. It was just possible they might think a timer switch in the computer controls had gone haywire. But I didn't hold out much hope for that –

We crept back to the studio. 'Problem,' murmured Demetria, frowning but perfectly cool. 'Don't worry, I can get us out. I'm going to create a diversion. Follow me, and be ready –'

She took something like a small, slim remote control out of one of her overall pockets. I didn't get a good look, because as soon as she started pushing buttons, the lights went out.

'Get down,' she hissed. 'Crawl!'

We were in complete blackness. Next moment, a sparse network of needle-fine red beams sprang into existence, about a metre off the ground. I was glad I'd dropped to the floor when Demetria told me to, because I had a feeling they weren't just pretty lights. I heard exclamations and cursing from the big room, where Doric and his goons must have been plunged into utter darkness as well. Demetria was using the flat's own high tech to cover our escape. She'd told me to follow, but I couldn't see her! I crawled to the door, or where I thought the door ought to be. I should have been very scared. I wasn't, not at the time. What was happening was too exciting. As I reached the door it opened. I crouched back, and as someone stepped past me playing a torch beam around the darkness I dived forward.

Then things got confusing. There was a rushing sound, like a waterfall. Someone was cursing: someone else was yelling in a foreign language, and blundering about falling over the furniture. Something (a machine of some kind) was bleeping madly in the kitchen. I saw a blurred figure outlined in a torch beam, waving what looked to me like a gun. I didn't know what had happened to Demetria, but there was a struggle going on, two bodies crashing and rolling about . . . The darkness seemed full of hot smoke.

I'd just realized that it wasn't smoke, it was *steam* from the bathroom, where the rushing sound was boiling hot water pouring out of the taps and the shower, when the lights came on again. I got to my feet (I put my hands in the air, I was afraid someone was going to shoot me). Two of the heavies who'd come in with Doric were fighting free of a big black-and-white rug. Demetria must have managed to throw it over them, that was the struggle I'd heard. Doric was standing in the middle of the room, in a cloud of steam, looking furious. It wasn't a gun in his hand, it was another of those remote-control things. He started to bark something like 'Get the kid!' but I shot past him, and though he'd got control of the lights again, the front door was standing wide open. One of the heavies tried to grab me from behind. I fought free and bolted. Demetria was with me, we were out in the passageway. She slammed the door behind us, fumbled for her lockpick gadget and pressed it against the cardslot. She had to do this one-handed, because in her other hand she was holding what seemed to be a real, small gun –

'There,' she gasped. 'I've scrambled the combination. That should hold them for a few minutes –' She started to run, I followed. We dashed through a door marked EMERGENCY EXIT and belted down flight after flight of concrete stairs, until we reached ground level.

'What are we going to do now?' I gasped.

'Walk out.'

The security guard was still behind his desk. There were no sirens going off, no flashing lights, the break-in on the top floor didn't seem to have registered down here. I don't know if he noticed that we'd left our toolbags behind. If he did, it didn't bother him.

Demetria's van was parked in the shadows where she'd left it. We jumped in and drove.

'Now do you believe me?' she said. 'And will you help me?'

We'd stopped in a quiet spot, at the other end of Beachcombe seafront. I'd climbed over into the back of the van, to get out of my disguise. 'I don't know what you want me to believe,' I protested. 'You haven't *told* me anything.' I wriggled out of the overalls, climbed back into the front and sat beside her, raising my eyebrows, waiting for the explanation.

'Was that a real gun?' I asked, when she said nothing.

She nodded.

'Would you have actually used it?'

She gave me a rueful half smile. 'I didn't expect us to get caught. We shouldn't have wasted time looking around. I'm sorry I put you in danger. But now you know, Mr Shelf-filler Alan. These people can get rough. So can I, if I have to. You've fallen into strange and risky company.'

'Are you going to tell me what's going on?'

She sighed. 'There's not much I can tell. I'm a private investigator. I got involved with NIMROD, or the people behind NIMROD, because ... someone disappeared. Disappeared like your sister, gone without a trace. That was the start of it. I've since found evidence that maybe a lot of people have disappeared. I want to know if it's true, and I want to know why it's happening. But however they manage it, they're good at keeping up a smoke screen. People who have become curious about NIMROD – or what lies behind NIMROD – don't always disappear, but they somehow melt away ... They're not around any more: can't be reached. Or else they suddenly change their minds. Suddenly there is no evidence, no mystery, no problem. But there *is* a problem, Alan. I can't tell you what's going on, because I don't *know* what's going on. But *the mystery is real.*'

'What about that cat? However they did it, why did they make a movie like that?'

'Probably for intimidation. A warning ...' She turned to me, urgently. It was almost dark inside the van. I could only imagine the look in her clear eyes, but I could hear the anger and sincerity in her voice. 'Alan, think about Stacey. What if your sister *is* alive? What if Stacey's in terrible danger, and I can help you to save her?'

'What is it you want me to do? I mean, suppose I believe any of this.'

'Nothing, yet. Just keep your eyes and ears open. And *be careful.*'

She dropped me off, not too near our house, saying, 'I'll be in touch.' I stood in the dark street, watching until the van turned a corner and was out of sight. 'Thanks for a great night out,' I said, aloud. I had a sore place on my chest where one of those red needle-beams had struck me a glancing blow. It was stinging and throbbing. This cannot be me, I was thinking. I cannot have broken into a luxury flat, with a beautiful private investigator who casually carries a gun. Not me, not Shelf-filler Alan.

How could Stacey have been kidnapped, from halfway up a cliff? *Could Stacey still be alive?* I didn't know whether to believe a word Demetria said. But I wanted to believe her. Was it because she excited me, because I wanted to be with her and join in her dangerous games? Or was it because I needed the incredible hope she offered me – needed it so much that I simply couldn't resist?

# Nine

*I* HAD A THIN STRIPE OF BLACK-AND-PURPLE BRUISE across my chest, a bad taste in my mouth from that hologram-movie clip of the cat; and a lot of questions that my friend Demetria couldn't or wouldn't answer. It was time to find out something more about NIMROD for myself. The famous Internet site seemed like the obvious place to start. I decided to enlist Caz, because I don't like messing with computers. I'm not technophobic, I just don't like 'em.

On Friday night we were ensconced in Jo's study, in front of his fancy fast PC, equipped with popcorn and Cola and other nibbles, all set for a surfing spree. According to our two-household routine, it was one of the weekends Mum would spend round here. Jo was supposed to be going to fetch her, but he was still hanging about: we'd banished him to the living room. About ten he put his head around the door. Caz was playing a game she'd found called CRASH. I was sitting behind her, munching snacks and offering advice.

'I'm off to meet Jackie,' he said. 'We'll be back around midnight, maybe a little later. Are you staying the night, Alan?'

'No.'

It was sort of a superstition. I didn't spend the night around here unless there was a special reason. Especially not on their weekends together. Maybe I was still a bit jealous of Jo with my mum. He sighed, and glanced across at the PC. 'What's that you're doing, Caz?'

'My homework.'

'Hmm. I see.' Not unless they were studying the effects of large-bore ammunition on human flesh, as their general science topic. Caz slapped a key as he came up for a closer look, and the screen defaulted to an encyclopedia page. Sometimes Jo looked as if bringing up a teenage girl was wearing him out. This was one of those nights.

'Okay, I'm off.' He grinned at me. 'I trust you to keep her under control, Alan.'

'No one can keep me under control,' growled Caz in her toughest voice.

'You can depend on me,' I said. Jo and I gripped hands, in male solidarity . . . a joke, but there was an odd moment then. He held on to my hand longer than he needed to, smiling down at me where I sat in his leather armchair. I'd never seen him look so sad and tired. 'And you can depend on me, Alan,' he said solemnly. 'I won't let you down. I promise.'

'What's up with him?' I asked, when we'd heard the front door close.

'Oh, who knows,' sighed Caz. 'Money trouble, work trouble, your mum – I think they've been rowing over the Stacey business again. He's a pig to live with just now, always in a bad mood. Got to be careful not to 'rass him for a while: he'll get over it.'

I privately thought she could have added *Caz* to that list of worries, but I didn't say so. Now that we were alone, it was time to talk NIMROD.

I'd told her nothing about the 'living ghost' sessions. I wasn't going to risk breaking Doric's rule of secrecy, until I understood what was going on. (I didn't know what Mum had told Jo, but that wasn't my business.) I'd simply told her I'd decided to look at the site but I didn't want my mum to know. She could understand that. She knew what it was like, living with the Search for Stacey.

We'd be using Mum's password, of course. But I was entitled to do that. Dittany had *wanted* me to get involved.

I'd been afraid that somehow they would know about me breaking into Doric's flat. But nothing had happened. Mum spent her days waiting, in hope and miserable suspense, to be summoned to another session. Dittany kept phoning up and promising that they were making great progress, and warning her not to talk to anyone, especially the media: but that was all so far. Now I was worried that NIMROD would spot that her password was being used on another machine, not the one at our house. I was afraid they'd know it was me that was using it without her, and they'd guess that I was getting nosey and suspicious. Caz laughed at this idea.

'That's science fiction, Alan. The NIMROD people aren't, like, looking through the screen into my dad's study, and reading the mind of the person who's hitting the keys. They *could* find out you're logging on from a different machine, but they can't know what's going through your head, don't be so daft. The software might get nasty and chuck us off, if it thinks we're misbehaving. But NIMROD will never know anything, long as we're a bit discreet.'

'Right,' I agreed. Caz habitually talked about 'the software' and 'the machine' and so on, as if they were people. It bemused me: maybe it was a generation gap. 'As long as you're sure.'

She keyed in the address I'd given her. Up came a black screen, with the stylized figure of an archer drawing a bow, etched in twinkling silver. The acronym, with the same jewelled look, was in big letters underneath. The twinkling letters kept morphing into little archers.

'It looks impressive,' said I.

'Standard stuff,' commented Caz scornfully. 'Let's see. Looks as if I click on the big figure.'

With Caz driving the mouse, moving the cursor and

clicking, and me peering over her shoulder, we progressed through screens full of the NIMROD history (all that guff about the US Army colonel). Then some corny testimonals from satisfied customers: and finally the front page of the chatsite. To me this was a confusing maze of bizarre instructions and little flashing boxes, but Caz had no problem. She entered Mum's password: Delia.

'Here we go!'

I was holding my breath. But nothing happened, no trouble at all. We were in.

So this was the fabled NIMROD site, where messages from lost souls all over the world, living and dead, were supposedly being captured by the magic of digital telecommunication. There was a black banner across the top of the screen, with a frieze of little stylized twinkling archers. Down the left side ran a panel with a list of names in it, all beginning with D. Apparently about fifteen NIMROD subscribers were on-line. On the main panel lines of type scrolled at a reading pace: some in red, some in green, occasionally one in purple, most in black. Caz, who had rapidly scanned the instructions, pointed helpfully. 'The red text is the software talking. See it's just told everyone on-line that *Delia has joined us*: that's us. The names in the left panel are the names of the NIMROD subscribers.'

'I worked out that much.'

'Their text comes up in green, with their spirit name at the start. It's like a play script, see? The speaker's name is on the left. The red lines with no name in front, they're like the stage directions. See the box at the bottom? Whatever we want to say, I type it and it appears in there, then I hit the enter key and it should come up on everybody's screen. If you want to say something to a particular person, you type "Delia speaks to Dogbiscuit", or whoever. Then the message is only seen by the person you named and by the moderator who's in charge tonight. That's the one whose lines come up in purple. But if this is like any other chatroom, that might be software too. The moderators are often not really human, they're just 'bots. There's more things you can do, but let's get chatting –'

'What about the black print?'

'Oh, *that*'s the messages from missing persons. If there's a "D" name in front it means the channellers think they've identified that person. You click on the "D" name, the spirit name: and if you have the right password the screen will show you whatever information NIM-ROD has about them, like their real name maybe, or where they are. Didn't you read the instructions?'

I'd tried. But those lines of print in boxes put my brain out of gear.

'What shall I put?' she demanded.

'Let me watch for a while.'


(no name): *Talk to me talk to me talk to me someone please talk to me*

Dorothea: *My name is Leonard Cohen, I write songs, I live in a tree*

Didymus: *I'm alone, I'm so alone. I remember your eyes, and our baby's smile*

(no name): *I'm sorry, I'm so sorry, for all the bad things I've done*

Dion: *Hi! I'm Dion, in Kansas City. I've been with NIMROD for three months, I'm looking for my husband. I just want to tell him please let us know you're okay –*


There didn't seem to be anyone making contact with their loved ones, or suspected loved ones. The print was mostly black and the few lines of green type just said 'Hello' basically. 'Hello, has anyone seen my husband . . .?' 'Hello, has anyone heard from my daughter?' Maybe we'd picked a bad night.

Jo's study was dark, we hadn't bothered to switch on

any lights. There was only the glow from the screen, and the soft hum of the PC's cooling system. The NIMROD messages flowed on, lost and sad. It was like watching a disaster in slow motion, that was happening far away. I imagined my mum sitting staring at this stuff by the hour, waiting for a line that was supposed to come from our Stacey's brain talking in its sleep . . .

'Internet chat is usually rubbish,' muttered Caz. 'But this is the creepiest I've seen. You know what I think? I think *all* the black-text people are dead. They think they're alive, just missing. Really they're rotting brains, in jars. NIMROD has these jars wired up to their main computer in a lab somewhere. That's why they're so confused and miserable because they're dead but they don't know it –'

'You've been watching too many sci-fi cartoons.'

'So, what shall I put? *Are you there, Stacey?* Would that do?' She giggled nervously. 'Look, there's poor old Leonard Cohen again. It's like watching for your luggage in an airport, isn't it. There's always stuff that gets left on the band. Round and round they go, the bags that nobody wants. Well, I'm sick of this. I'm going to type something –'

'No! Don't you dare type anything. Get off the keyboard.' There was a slight scuffle, Caz having the dumb idea that she could keep me from taking over. I didn't need to use much force, I'm a bit big for that. But when I'd taken her place, I just gazed at the screen. She was right, there was something deeply creepy about those silent cries for help. The black lines scrolled by. Was there anybody there, out in 'the aether'. Or was it all a trick? Suddenly – I don't know what made me do it – my fingers hit the keys.

*Where is my sister?*

I smacked the enter key, and there were my words, transported to the NIMROD dimension. In the next line, as if in reply, *I'm alone, I'm so alone . . .* came up again.

Caz groaned impatiently. 'I take it back about the brains in the jars, I think it's a plain fake. The NIMROD moderator is sitting somewhere making up all those black-type messages. Probably not even making them up, probably got a little program going to deliver "random miserable messages". Then when someone like your mum logs on they add something personalized from the Stacey file.'

'Channeller,' I said. 'Not moderator. They're called channellers.' Caz was a smart kid. The set-up was probably pretty much precisely as she'd described it. But I went on staring, half hypnotized. As if, like Mum, I still believed although I *knew* it was a con . . . It was a few minutes before I managed to wrench myself free. I let her in front of the keyboard again. 'Close it down. I've seen enough.'

All I'd found out was that the NIMROD site was exactly what I'd expected. A sad fake.

'Well, hey. That's funny,' said Caz.

'What's funny?'

'I got a glimpse of their stats. Guess how many live subscribers have visited the NIMROD site, 'cording to this?'

'Haven't a clue.'

'Fifty-seven.'

'Is that a lot?'

'No, it isn't! That's *pathetic*, Alan. Popular sites get, like, hundreds of thousands of hits a day. Fifty-seven is ridiculous. That could be . . . that could be just your mum, logging on to try and talk to Stacey.'

'It probably *is* just my mum. You probably saw the number of hits for her password. Either that, or you misread it.'

'No, no. It was fifty-seven, and it was for the whole site!'

She couldn't prove it. The screen on which she'd glimpsed this magic number refused to reappear. She went on trying, typing in different bits of the NIMROD address to see what would come up, and muttering under her breath about html indexes, IP addresses and other weird terms. She was annoyed, because she loved showing off to me about how clever she was with computers.

I let her go on, but she needn't have bothered. I'd already seen enough to start me thinking. Those messages, so vague and meaningless: those few lines from 'real live subscribers' . . . All of it could easily be the work of one NIMROD channeller: such as that old witch Dittany. I was remembering that none of Mum's netfriends on the missing persons circuit had heard of NIMROD . . .

Supposing this site had been set up purely for Mum's benefit? Set up like a real chatsite, with the usual features? That might mean the software would do things NIMROD didn't want it to do, like counting the number of times the site was used by actual, genuine subscribers. But maybe you could fix it so only a nosey kid like Caz would snag that information.

They didn't think an ignorant, gullible grieving sucker like my mum would notice any revealing flaws. They were wrong. My mum knew. She knew she was probably dealing with crooks, but she didn't care . . . This much, I had known already. But if the *whole thing* had been set up to fool *my mum*, that meant Demetria was right. We were dealing with something more than a dodgy missing persons agency. I suddenly felt angry, angry and frightened. What were we getting into?

'Caz, stop that! Switch off the machine.'

It didn't make sense, but the monitor screen had started to look like a cold, inhuman face. As if someone back at NIMROD headquarters really was watching us, reading our minds. Caz powered down and switched off without giving me an argument.

'Did you find out anything else?'

'Well, their server, that's like the main computer that

puts NIMROD on the net, belongs to a company called Kaplan Communications. Have you heard of them?'

'No –' But my mind was leaping ahead. I already knew what I was going to do next.

Caz grabbed a handful of popcorn, stuffed it in her face and chewed, her eyes bright. As soon as she could speak she burst out: 'You're going after them, aren't you! You have to let me in on this. You need me, I'm good at computer stuff. You wouldn't have got anywhere tonight on your own.'

'This isn't computer stuff, Caz. That's a distraction. The truth is in the real world.'

'Then I want to be in on whatever you're planning in the real world.' She laughed. 'You know what, Alan? You look completely different when you're interested in something. You look like you've come back to life. Your grub-like brain's started to crawl out from under that stone where it usually lives.'

'Thanks a lot.'

But she was right. I felt different. More alive, more *real*, than I had been since that day.

Well, I argued with her, but my heart wasn't in it. I was hungry for human company. I'd been shut up in my own miserable world for so long; and I wasn't planning to do anything dangerous, only look around and ask a few questions. Next day, Saturday, I had a day off. We met in town. We weren't exactly in disguise, but we were wearing our oldest clothes. I was planning to visit The Casbah, that restaurant where Mum's first NIMROD meeting had been held, and I knew those streets around the station were not the place to be strutting your latest labels. I had also found myself a very dodgy hat – an old cricket hat that had belonged to my dad – so that no one could get a good look at my face.

We walked up from the town-centre bus stop together, me and Caz – away from the seafront with its bright summer crowds, into the sadlands. The respectable visitors probably didn't know, or they didn't think, about this side of life in Beachcombe. They passed the beggars outside the station forecourt, they saw the tumbledown buildings and the figures slumped in doorways: and off they went, down the hill into the sunshine. But a lot of drifters end up at the seaside, partly because there's casual work in the tourist trade, partly because there's nowhere further to go. Every resort has its bad patches. This was one of ours.

'What are we going to do?' demanded Caz.

'I'm not sure. I'll decide when we get there.'

She rolled her eyes and giggled. 'It's Alan Robarts,' she intoned. 'But not as we know him!'

I was getting irritated with this line. I knew what I was going to do: I simply wasn't going to tell Caz. I was wishing it could be Demetria beside me, with her cool, tawny-grey eyes and that touch of something wild. My chirpy wannabe kid-sister was a poor substitute.

It was about one o'clock. The evening that I'd brought Mum here there had been bright lights in The Casbah, appetizing smells and a busy atmosphere. It looked different by daylight. On one side of it was a shabby guesthouse. On the other side was a second-hand comic shop, the window full of yellowing, dog-eared stacks of pulp magazines. A fly-spotted notice said ADULT MATERIAL INSIDE. There was a man sitting on the doorstep. He seemed to be asleep, with a flat cap pulled down over his eyes, hands buried in the pockets of an ancient tweed jacket and his skinny knees drawn up to his chin.

'You stay here,' I said to Caz. We were surveying this scene from across the road.

A tapered pillar of doner-kebab meat turned slowly behind the greasy counter. In the display cabinet under it, bins of tired salad lay wilting. There seemed to be no one at home except for a tabby cat curled up on a chair and a young man, wearing a dirty apron over jeans and T-shirt, who was slouched at one of the tables reading a newspaper. I walked in. When I'd come with Mum there'd been music playing, and as far as I remembered every table had been full. Where were those happy customers now? Had *they* been part of the con? The young man looked up. He gave a start, and swiftly hid his newspaper under the table.

'You want kebab?' he grinned hopefully.

'No, I'm not feeling suicidal today.'

'Heh?'

'This is what I want.'

I did the NIMROD signs, quick and sly. I'd been practising.

The kebab man's grin vanished. He stared at me. I repeated the signs.

'Wha' you on about? I don' understand. You playin' fool with me?'

Suddenly he came at me in a rush, grabbed me by the arm and hustled me out of the door.

It slammed behind me. A hand flipped over the sign from OPEN to CLOSED, and a curtain was jerked across the glass. Caz zoomed over the street.

'*Now* will you tell me what you're hoping to achieve?'

'Shut up, I'm thinking.'

Maybe the doner-kebab seller was short-tempered, but it certainly seemed as if the NIMROD signs meant something to him. So The Casbah was more than an innocent venue they hired for their meetings. There was some real connection with NIMROD. I had only meant to try the signs and ask a few questions, but now I was convinced there must be some clue in there that would lead me to the little girl who was supposed to be Stacey. I was determined to get back inside. But how? I wasn't equipped for burglary today.

Caz said, in a puzzled voice, 'Alan, I think that beggar wants to speak to you.'

The man from the comic shop doorway was standing beside us. I suddenly realized he'd been there all along, watching what went on between me and the kebab-seller. He wasn't very old. His unshaven face was grimy pale and razor-thin. His right hand, when he saw that I was looking at him, briefly touched his forehead: both hands came together in front of his chest, and then sprang apart –

'Caz,' I snapped. 'Take a walk. You can go to the café on the corner and wait for me if you like. Or you can go home. But this is where you drop out. *Just do it.*'

I should have been suspicious when she didn't protest, but I was too interested in the beggar. Caz walked off: I quickly did the signs.

'Who are you?' I demanded. 'What do you know?'

He led the way around the back of the block, into a narrow alley. Still without a word he smiled, showing black and broken teeth, and began to haul at a pile of rubbish-spewing boxes. I stepped back, and nearly fell over Caz.

'I told you to take a walk!'

'I *did*. Just not a very long walk.'

I gave up. I knew Caz wouldn't go quietly, and I couldn't bear to miss this chance.

'What's going on?' she hissed.

'I don't know.'

The pile of boxes came apart easily and neatly. They'd looked messy, but they must have been carefully arranged. Behind them was a door. He opened it and pointed, nodding and smiling with his dreadful teeth: we were to go in. So in we went. We heard, as we stood staring around what seemed to be a storage cupboard, the dragging and thumping sounds of the rubbish barricade being replaced.

There were shelves around us, piled with dusty plates, boxes of paper napkins, glasses.

'Who was that?'

'I don't know.' But I was working it out. Had I seen a flicker of recognition in the eyes of that guy in the restaurant? Maybe, maybe not. Whichever, he'd certainly been warned not to answer questions from strangers, even if they knew the signs. But the message apparently hadn't got through to all the NIMROD underlings. Their guard on the back entrance thought we were okay. We'd better hope the two of them didn't get together while Caz and I were in here . . . 'If you know the signs, he lets you into The Casbah,' I said aloud. 'Through the secret back entrance. That's his job. We're supposed to know what to do next. If we know the signs, we're supposed to know what to do.'

'*What* signs?'

'Never mind. Something I can't tell you.'

She pulled a horrible face, but didn't insist. 'What's this got to do with NIMROD?'

'I don't know.'

On this side, the door that we'd come in by looked like a wall of the storage closet. There was another door, opposite. Caz opened it a crack and we glimpsed, through a big kitchen and a bead curtain, the domain of the greasy-apron guy who had chucked me out.

'Not that way,' I whispered. 'There's got to be somewhere else we can go. Otherwise what would be the point of letting us in here?'

The shelves didn't look hopeful. I took a closer look at the floor, which was covered in layers of old newspaper. I discovered that under the top layer there was a square patch in the middle that came up all of a piece, revealing a dark hole and a flight of steps.

Caz was thrilled. 'Hey! A secret passage!'

At the bottom of the steps I felt around and found a switch. A light came on, a bare bulb dangling on a piece of white plastic cable. We were in a passageway, with doors on either side. The walls had been painted white, recently. The surface was still faintly tacky when I touched it. Remembering the fancy flat down on the Marina, I checked for surveillance gadgets but I couldn't see anything: no wires, no threatening little boxes on the walls, no camera eyes in the ceiling. We began to explore, without saying much.

It was quiet down in those cellars, and bare; and chill. The first room we looked into was completely empty. The second was long and low. The dusty floor had odd, rectangular marks in two rows down the sides. I couldn't think what they were, until I saw at the end a pile of things like large grey sausage rolls, tied with string. Camping mattresses. Who had been sleeping down here, and why? There was nothing to explain it.

We kept finding light-switches, switching them on ahead and switching them off behind us. There were more piles of rolled mattresses, and more marks where they'd been laid out on the floors. There were no other signs of life, but the air smelled of disinfectant. It was like the aftermath of a disaster, like an air-raid shelter where all the huddling people had been vaporized. The cellars went on and on. Caz started to walk closer to me.

'I wonder what happened to them,' she muttered. 'All the people. Who were they? And where are we heading? We've been going downhill for ages, have you noticed? We must be practically under the sea.'

I was thinking about NIMROD, trying to get a handle on what I knew. Who *was* Doric anyway? With his beautiful flat and his bodyguards and his futuristic technology. If he was so rich and so clever, why was he going to all this trouble to con my mum?

Where did my lost little sister fit in to all this?

Where did *anything* fit in?

'I think this place is haunted,' whispered Caz. 'Don't you think so? Don't you think it feels haunted? Like, full of shadows you can't see? I bet the people who were sleeping on those mattresses have all been killed and eaten by the NIMROD gang. It's probably *their* brains in the jars . . . Yeah, that's it. They're the rotting brains that do the sad, weird talking on the NIMROD chatsite.'

'Shut up, Caz. Don't be stupider than you can help –'

We had reached a dead end, a room with no doors except the one we'd come in by.

'Now what?' said Caz.

She started to rap on the walls, looking for secret passages. I stood there feeling let down and puzzled; and more oppressed by the creepy, dank emptiness than I cared to admit. Like the rest, this room was freshly painted: but that didn't tell me anything.

'Hey, listen! It's wood, not brick behind here. I think there's a panel that moves –'

She was right. There seemed to be a sliding panel, made of hardboard. We found the join and pried and tugged. Suddenly it came free. Caz and I leapt away, as a heap of bodies, arms and legs, feet and hands and heads, came tumbling out from behind the wall –

Of course, they weren't really bodies. It only seemed that way.

We looked down at a huge heap of clothes and personal belongings, spilling over the cellar floor. There were jackets and trousers, pairs of shoes: skirts, dresses, underwear, spectacles, socks, worn handbags and wallets gaping open and empty. Everything looked shabby, and creased and stale. Jackets and dresses still held the shape of the bodies that had been inside them. A smell rose up: the sour dregs of unwashed human warmth.

Nothing to be afraid of. Nothing but a pile of old clothes.

It reminded me of a documentary I'd seen about the Second World War. It was like one of those piles of clothes found heaped up outside the gas chambers, in the death camps. I remembered that according to Demetria, NIMROD – or whatever was behind NIMROD – had a way of making people disappear.

'Looks like a lot of missing persons,' whispered Caz. 'I wonder where the bodies are.'

I was trying not to wonder about that myself. 'It's a bunch of old clothes, Caz.'

'Yeah, sure. But it's *spooky*.'

I picked up a piece of paper that was sticking out of an inside pocket of one of the jackets. It was a half page torn from a ringpull notebook. In the middle of a lot of squiggles – nothing like any language I could think of – two English words caught my eye: *Diamond Life*. I knew I'd seen those words before, and recently.

'Now we'd better stuff it all back.'

'Yuck! I don't want to touch them!'

'Yeah, well, I don't want anyone to know we've been snooping around.'

'I want to get out of here. I don't like this place. Alan, I don't think you should investigate NIMROD any more. I think you should tell my dad, or someone.'

'Tell him what? He knows. He told me he's investigated NIMROD, and it's harmless.'

'Yeah, maybe that's what he thought. But now we've found a *secret hiding place* where masses of people have been stripped naked and, and *done away with* somehow –'

'Look, you wanted to come along. So you came along. You insisted on following me when I told you to beat it. When are you going to learn to mind your own business?'

'Oh, so now I'm a useless kid. But who found out about Kaplan Communications?'

'Miaow?'

We both spun around. A cat came stepping into the room. For a moment Caz and I stared at it, bewildered. 'It's the cat from the restaurant,' I said. 'I saw it in the restaurant.'

Now it was on its feet, I could see that it was tabby and white, not plain tabby. I stared, fascinated. Those tabby-and-white markings looked awfully familiar.

'What's the matter, Alan?' wondered Caz. 'It's just a cat. It must have followed us.'

But I had shut the hatch in that storage closet behind me. Someone must have opened it. We both realized what this meant at the same moment: spun around and started to scrabble madly at the panelled wall. 'Listen!' wailed Caz. 'I can hear footsteps!' I could hear them too, coming closer. There had to be a way out! We stumbled in the tide of dirty clothes, our fear and disgust forgotten: and at last there it was, a dark opening. The cat darted ahead of us. We followed it along a narrow dark passageway to a door that was bolted on the inside. I fought with the bolt, we stepped out into a small paved yard: and were engulfed in sunlight. It was the back yard of another restaurant; Italian, this time, by the smells that came wafting over us. We could hear the clamour of the funfair on the seafront, over the clash of crockery from the kitchen. Someone was doing the washing up, and singing in a loud, high, mournful voice.

The cat had disappeared. The yard had a solid metal gate, padlocked shut and decorated along the top with barbed wire and spikes. I jumped on to a wheelie bin that was standing against this gate, hauled Caz up beside me and then swung her bodily up till she could get a foot between the spikes. She dropped out of sight (leaving a piece of trouser leg behind). I followed her. We landed in an alley, clothes torn but otherwise unhurt, and ran for it.

A few minutes later we were standing on the esplanade. The stream of brightly dressed people parted as it approached us, the crowd instinctively drawing away as if we were a dog's mess, or a patch of the sadlands, transported to a world where we didn't belong . . . We were filthy, and the dank, sour smell of those cellars was clinging to both of us. We didn't belong here . . . I was thinking about the cat. I was certain it was the same animal. I was absolutely sure I had seen the same tabby-

and-white cat starring in Doric's home movie clip, losing one of its nine lives in very messy style. If I'd looked under the fur, would I have found the scars from where its head had been torn apart? Pity we'd let it go . . .

'What are we going to do now, Al?' demanded Caz. 'Al? Hey, Al?'

'It was the cat. It was the same cat . . .'

'The same as what?'

'Nothing. I can't tell you.'

I needed to talk to someone, someone other than Caz. I was going to send her home, and make it stick this time. But I looked at her anxious, dirty face, and I suddenly thought: it was *her* future too, hanging in this balance. Her life, like mine, was trapped in limbo by the Search for Stacey. 'Come on. We're going to visit a friend of mine,' I said.

Mo lived in a block of single-bedroomed council flats. It wasn't anything much to look at, but it was clean and respectable. We stopped off at the friendly discount store on the corner of his street. I always brought something when I went to visit Mo. It was a ritual that we both appreciated. I let Caz choose the cakes: three boxes of leading-brand fancies for a pound. A good deal, so long as it didn't bother you that they were well past their best-by date.

Mo's place was on the fourth floor, with a tiny balcony where he was growing tomatoes, and a view over the streets to the sea. He was at home when we knocked. He didn't go out much. He knew Caz from her visits to Countryfare, but this was the first time they'd been formally introduced. He made the tea, I collected the crockery together and Caz, as the youngest and greediest, got the privilege of setting out the cakes. We sat down together, Caz and I on the bed that doubled as a sofa, Mo arranged in the strange way he sits to get comfortable, draped like a spider over his single armchair. Besides the bed and that chair there wasn't much else in the room, except for cardboard boxes full of second-hand books. You could guess, from the lack of possessions, the kind of drifting life he'd led. But now he had a home, and he seemed contented to me. The windows were open. We could hear the cockatiels that lived next door whistling and chirruping to each other; the TVs through the building were blaring out Saturday sport.

'These cakes are great,' said Caz. 'I'm going to bring Dad round here to do the week's shopping. Then he could stop fretting about his overdraft. Or whatever it is that's bugging him. I'm sick of the old bear. He's never home, and if he is home he does nothing but sit in his study brooding. Actually it's probably not money, it's probably Al's mum –'

Mo liked to see Caz eat, I could tell. Occasionally he'd reach out and shift the plate around – it was a pink plate, with chipped gilt around the edges and a pattern of roses – to get her a new angle on the tasties. But he was watching me too, with a concerned look on his twisted face. He knew this wasn't a social call.

'Mo,' I began at last. 'How do you know when to trust someone?'

It wasn't what I'd meant to say, but was the right thing. I needed to tell someone about what had been happening. My dead sister alive again. The luxury flat on the Marina, full of science-fiction gadgets. A missing persons agency with an Internet site set up, by people we'd never met or heard of until a few weeks ago, specifically to deceive *my mother*. A cellar full of old clothes ... But it was Demetria, most of all. The rest of it I either couldn't tell him or it wouldn't make sense. The only thing I really needed to know was whether or not I could trust her. If I could trust Demetria, I thought I could handle everything else.

'If someone lets me down badly, once,' said Mo, after giving it some thought, 'I don't rely on them again.'

'What, *never?*' I suppose I sounded distressed by this verdict: I was.

'As a rule of thumb,' explained Mo, 'it works. I've found that out the hard way.' He gave me his wonky smile, full of curiosity and wise sympathy. 'Course,' he added, 'you can like someone, you can even *love* someone, that you wouldn't trust further than the street corner. I've found that out too –'

'What's this got to do with NIMROD?' asked Caz. 'Someone's conning Alan's mum, that's the main thing. They're trying to convince her they've found his lost little sister. And there's something weird about a cat,' she told him, around a mouthful of elderly Battenburg. 'I'm sure the cat's very important. But he wouldn't explain why.'

I'd told her to call Mo 'Mr Doyle'.

'Tell her to call me Mo,' he said. He knew Caz must be having difficulty understanding him. 'What's this about a con trick?'

'It's an organization,' said Caz, cheerfully taking over my story. 'Called NIMROD. They're pretending they're getting messages from Alan's sister Stacey, the one who disappeared. It's so strange! They've got a site set up on the Internet, a sort of missing persons bulletin board. We think it was created just for Alan's mum, but why would anyone go to that much trouble?'

'I don't know about the Internet,' said Mo, looking interested. 'But I know how con-men work, if you mean the professionals. You've hit the nail on the head. That's just what they want you to think. *Why would anyone go to so much trouble?* You know why people get fooled by con artists? It's because they can't believe anyone would put so much work into setting up a false story, with all the details and the props, and the acting. But to the professionals that's the game, you see. It's for their own satisfaction, they *enjoy* deceiving people.'

'Yes, but –' I tried to break in, but Mo was on a roll.

'Keep your eye on the ball. That's my best advice. If

someone shows you something that *has to be* fake, you just remember it *has to be fake*, and don't let anyone change your mind with flim-flam work.'

'Yes, but you don't understand. I've seen things I just *can't* explain.'

Caz was concentrating on the cakes: I suppose she couldn't follow much of what Mo was saying once he got going. Mo was shaking his head, in a pitying way. It was like one of our Countryfare conversations: my turn to be the believer, his turn to be the sensible, sceptical one. Suddenly I remembered the piece of paper I'd picked up in that cellar. I wanted to ask him did he recognize the writing, did he know what language it was? Mo had a great fund of strange bits of knowledge. I searched my pockets, unfolded the half sheet and found myself looking at the words *Diamond Life*.

Now I remembered where I'd seen them before! *And I remembered something else.*

Something dazzling!

'Thanks for the advice, Mo,' I said. 'I'm sure you're right. I wish I could see a way to convince my mum, that's all.'

Mo looked disappointed. I wasn't supposed to cave in like that . . . But I didn't want to talk about NIMROD any more. I wanted to get away. I made an excuse as soon as I could, and – after shaking off Caz with some difficulty – headed home.

I was surprised to find Mum there. She was supposed to be round at Jo's. Something had happened, obviously: maybe they'd had a row, because she was looking miserable. But she didn't explain, and I was too preoccupied to pay much attention. We ate together – pasta with sauce out of a jar, we're neither of us interested in cooking – then I told her I was going out, and I might be late back. She reminded me that I had to be up early for work tomorrow. (I liked working Sundays instead of Saturdays. Sunday was a nice quiet day at Countryfare.)

Since I'd left Mo's, I'd been wondering wildly how I was going to get back into that flat down at the Marina. I had no secret-agent skills, and no gadget to open electronic locks. Over the pasta it had dawned on me that I didn't need to break in. I could get another look inside without any trouble at all. I took a bus down to the sea, and presented myself at the gates of that luxury housing compound. The eye of a security camera looked down. I didn't care. I had nothing to hide.

When the garbled voice on the entryphone asked me my business, I said, 'Alan Robarts, to see Mr Kaplan.'

That would show him. Mr Doric NIMROD Kaplan, who thought my mum and I were so dumb, so easily fooled. I felt angry and proud. If I was right . . . But I was sure I was right.

I wasn't going to confront him. Far from it. But I thought Doric would be interested to see me. He'd want to know where I got his address, where I found the name Kaplan. I would simply explain, innocently, that I'd looked up this information on the Internet. That would show him. Then I'd pretend I'd come to ask him in private, man to man, away from Mum, what did he *really* think of our chances of locating my sister. I was sure I could convince him that I was still a willing victim of the NIMROD scam. We were supposed to be idiots, weren't we? The important thing was to get back inside for a few minutes.

There was a short silence, then the lock clicked and buzzed, the gates came open. First round to me. A few moments later I'd passed the security desk and I was in the lift.

Mr Doric Kaplan himself let me in. He stood in the doorway, dapper and smiling.

'Hello, Alan,' he said. 'This is a surprise. Come in, sit down, tell me all about it.'

'I hope you don't mind me coming here, Mr Doric. It's about my mum.'

He didn't ask how I'd found his address, or how I'd known to call him 'Mr Kaplan' on the entryphone. He didn't ask me anything. That should have made me suspicious. But I was full of wild excitement, because of what I had remembered. So I sat there without a qualm, going on about how my mum was, and how the hope NIMROD had given her was tearing her apart (true enough), and could he tell me, in private, whether they were getting anywhere? Doric was drinking Sepporo beer. He offered me a drink, and fetched me a Coke himself. He seemed to be alone in the flat this evening. He sat back on a plushy sofa, his small neat feet on the rug that Demetria had thrown over the two heavies on my first, unofficial visit. His hands, which were small too, and stubby-fingered, kept patting that thin crust of ginger hair, and playing with a signet ring on his left little finger. He said things like: *I know how hard it is* . . . and *you have to be patient* . . . and *I can't promise quick results but there's every reason to hope* . . .

When he started looking at his watch, I said I'd better be going. I thanked him for talking to me, and told him he'd made me feel a lot better. I asked if I could use the bathroom.

Of course he said yes. I even remembered – just! – to ask him where it was. I set off to use the bathroom, and then (having used it, quite genuinely) left that door shut and the light inside on, while I sneaked on tiptoe along the passage to the studio. I slipped inside. Everything was the same as it had been: the mixing desks, the futuristic equipment, the black walls, the central table. The silver ashtray with the words *Diamond Life* on the rim. But there was something else. In here, there was no expensive-looking modern art. The decorations on the walls were framed colour photographs of boats. Big boats, gleaming on blue sea. Which was natural enough, considering that we were overlooking the yacht basin.

I stood looking at the photograph, the one that had caught my eye.

My heart sank. Excitement had fooled me. There was no way I could be completely sure. *But I knew.* This was the same boat, the motor yacht that had been passing between Beachcombe Marina and The Islands, one afternoon in May three years ago. This was the connection between what had happened to my sister Stacey, and NIMROD. The name of the yacht was printed under its portrait.

*The Diamond Life.*

Something moved behind me. I spun around. Mr Doric Kaplan, still smiling, was at the door. 'Did you get lost, Alan?' he asked gently.

'This is a terrific place you have here, Mr Doric,' I managed to say, in my most grovelling tone. 'I bet you get an incredible sound from all this hi-fi.'

'You bet I do.'

Smiling, he waited as I left the studio, falling over my own feet in my nervousness. Smiling, he escorted me into the hallway and watched until the lift doors closed.

I went and sat on a bollard in the car park outside the Marina supermarket, out of sight and weak-kneed with relief. That had been close. I hoped he'd think I couldn't resist sneaking a little look around. A kid like me in a fancy pad like that, it was natural wasn't it? I hoped he believed I'd mistaken the video-mixing equipment for hi-fi . . .

'Hi, Alan.'

I started. *Caz* was standing there, dressed in black, with her puffa jacket and her kappas, looking insufferably pleased with herself.

'What are you doing here?' I demanded.

'I *followed* you,' she explained proudly. 'It was the way you behaved at Mo's place, Alan. You ought to see a face-trainer or something. You took me to see Mr Doyle, we started talking about NIMROD, and suddenly you got this expression on your face like: ALAN HAS A BIG IDEA! Then you didn't want to be with us any more. You rushed me out and sent me home. I don't know what your friend Mo thought, but I *knew* there was something up. So I came round to your house, and watched until you came out. I got on the bus to the Marina behind you, and you never saw me! So, now you're going to have to tell me what's going on, aren't you!'

I heard a loud clang. I saw, way behind Caz, a man in dark clothes who had sent a supermarket trolley racing across the tarmac, into the corral at the end of a row of parking slots. The man looked at me. I couldn't see his face clearly, but it was pointing straight in my direction. He was big, muscle-bound, and I had seen him before –

'Alan? What's the matter? What's happened, have you turned into a zombie?'

She was waving her hand in front of my face. I grabbed her wrist.

'Caz, get out of here,' I snapped. 'Go on, scoot. Keep out of my business.'

'Oh no!' She laughed. 'Not a chance, Alan. You know, you still owe me –'

I was breaking out in a sweat. How could I save her? 'Look, Caz, I'm on to something, okay? But I need to do this alone. I want you to go home, and stay by a telephone. I might need help in a hurry. Can you do that?'

She grinned in triumph. 'I don't have to go home. I've got my dad's mobile, I nicked it from his jacket. I'll wait for you here. Where are you going?'

'Caz, will you GET OUT OF HERE. I am sick of being followed around by a stupid little thirteen-year-old kid. CLEAR OFF!'

Caz backed off a pace. Her face fell, hard. I thought she was going to burst into tears. 'I am not thirteen,' she said in a hurt and shocked voice. 'I'm fourteen, can't you even remember how old I am? I know you're getting in bad trouble, you're my brother and *I love you –*'

Then she bolted, to my great relief.

There were three of them now. They were strolling casually towards me, as if they expected me to wait for them, like a good boy. Wait and see what Mr Kaplan's heavies wanted to say. I left it as long as I dared. Then I jumped up and belted off in the opposite direction from Caz. I ran through the car park, over the concrete apron at the entrance to the Marina, and vaulted over the sea wall. The drop wasn't much. I started to run, back towards Beachcombe and the lights and the evening crowds.

The tide was out, the sea was a silky grey scarf flung between me and the horizon. I was doing well. But soon the hard sand ran out and I was struggling through shingle. I'm not a good runner. The hefty figures were nearer every time I turned my head, and they hadn't made my mistake. Two of them had stayed up on the concrete, only one of them was down on the beach to block my retreat. The gap was closing fast. Now I was running in my nightmare: the persistent nightmare of those first weeks after Stacey had vanished. The shingle trapped my feet, my lungs were burning. I wasn't going to make it and, the same as in the dream, I couldn't scream, I couldn't shout.

In the end I was running without hope of escape, because you can't give in. A hand fell on my shoulder, and gripped like iron. I thought of that metal band around the cat's head. The hand turned me around, blurred faces stared at me. Some kind of stocking masks . . . A fist came out of the dusk, and hit my jaw so hard I thought my neck had snapped.

When I woke up, the room I was lying in was moving gently. I didn't move or open my eyes, because I had a feeling it would hurt too much. Lucky I didn't. The next moment I heard voices, and I became aware that two people – at least two people – were standing looking down at me.

'Why don't we knock him on the head and chuck him over the side?' The voice was thin and reedy, with an odd accent: maybe disguised.

'Water,' croaked the other. I recognized the old witch Dittany's harsh tones at once. 'In the lungs.'

'Huh?'

'He has to be breathing when he drowns or it won't look accidental. And we don't want him to turn up too soon. This is the way to do it.'

A door closed with a heavy clunk. I was left alone.

Some time later – could have been minutes or hours, I was very woozy – the door to the cabin opened again. I sat up on the narrow bunk where I was lying. A stranger came in, a thin little guy in sailor's gear with a dark mask over his face, and wearing gloves. He had a look at the bruise on the side of my jaw, which was cut and bleeding; and gave me a mug of hot coffee. 'What's going on?' I demanded. 'Where am I?'

He left without a word.

I started calling for help. After a while someone came and spoke through the cabin door. It was the voice with the strange accent. It said I should drink coffee, go to sleep and everything would be explained soon. I didn't know if I was being watched. So I tried to look as if I was drinking the coffee, while actually I was pouring it down behind the cushions, to be soaked up by the bedding on the bunk. Then I tried to look like someone falling deeply asleep. Best I could think of to do.

# Ten

*I* WAS SURE THE COFFEE HAD BEEN DRUGGED. MAYBE I swallowed some when I was pretending to drink it, or maybe it was the after-effects of that smack on the head. Anyway, I really *did* fall asleep, or I drifted into unconsciousness. I half woke, sometime later, aware that I was being carried. There was musty heavy cloth over my face and roped around my body. I tried not to give any sign of life. There was the sound of an engine, a lot of jolting and swinging around; no voices. Then everything was quiet again.

Gradually I came fully awake. I was lying on something cold and hard. My head was pounding, my neck hurt and I felt sick. But I wasn't tied up any more. I struggled until the rough matting that was wrapped round me came loose and fell away. At first I thought I was still on that boat. I could hear a lapping sound, and when I looked up I could see, through the gloomy, blueish half-dark, water ripples of light and shadow shifting, far overhead . . .

I was alone in a long cubicle of grey-painted metal, with slatted partition walls, benches along the sides and rows of hooks above them. I stood up and crept, helping myself along by the wall like a very old man, to the door, which was a swinging flap of metal. Pushing it aside, I saw I was in the first of a row of these sort of 'changing rooms', all with the same benches, lockers underneath them and hooks above. Looking the other way I saw a big rectangular pool of water. There was a grey deck around it, lit by dim bulkhead lights in metal cages. I saw heavy fenders slung along the waterside: and at the far end of the pool a blank barrier. I seemed to be in some kind of big boathouse; empty at the moment. Was I still on the Marina? When I stared at the reflected ripples overhead, I could see beyond them a vaulted roof of rock: rugged natural chalk. It looked as if a natural cavern had been enlarged, a cave in the chalk cliffs.

Then I knew where I must be. Then I understood . . . at least part of it. I crept back to my bench. I felt cold, so cold. I pulled the dirty matting around me and hid my face.

Why did I go back to that flat on my own? I must have been crazy. But that was me, Alan Robarts, all over. Every day of my life, until the day my little sister vanished, I used to be in some kind of trouble. I was always the one to take a risk, to act first and regret it later. I remembered Caz saying I'd woken up, I'd come back to life. I should have stayed under my stone. I should have kept on being zombie Alan, shelf-filler Alan, waiting-to-die Alan. My little sister had disappeared because somehow she'd found this secret place. Now I was going to vanish too, taken out and dropped over the side of a boat without a chance of rescue: and I still had *no idea* why these things had happened. That was the worst thing. I was going to be killed and I was never even going to know why.

You do something that you know is a bit dodgy. Like spending your bus fare in a games arcade, like trying to walk home with your little sister against the rising tide. Like knocking on the door of a guy you know is some serious kind of villain, and calling him by his right name: telling him that his cover is blown. Why? It seems like a good idea at the time. Then you look back when everything is in ruins, and you have no one to blame but yourself.

I don't know how long I lay there, huddled in my matting, full of misery. I was roused from an aching doze by the sound of footsteps. Some people, two or three, I couldn't be sure, were in the locker room next to mine. I heard voices. I rolled over, trying not to make a sound, and peered through the slats in the partition wall.

I saw Dittany. The old witch was dressed in navy-blue slacks and a chunky white sweater, very nautical and natty, with the usual black bird's-nest hairdo and heavy make-up. She was standing by a small metal table, talking to someone out of my sight. A curl of blue smoke drifted from beside her: I could smell tobacco.

'Now, let's have a look at it. See what needs to be fixed . . . Stacey?' she croaked in a different tone. 'Where are you, pet? Come on, little ghost. Come to Mother!'

I'd seen the studio in Kaplan's flat. I knew there was nothing supernatural going on. But my skin crept. A shadow appeared a few metres away from Dittany, hovering above the floor. It thickened, it grew into the shape of a little girl in a shabby tracksuit with tousled yellow-brown hair: the child that we'd seen, Mum and I, in that upper room at The Maypole and in an empty suburban living room. But this time she was crouching in a huddled heap, hiding her face.

I remembered what the girl in the NIMROD sessions had told us: *I'm in the grey place . . .*

'Now, Stacey, what's happened to you? Tell us what's happening, eh?'

'Please, don't do that, please, don't do that. Oh the poor thing, the poor thing . . .'

She sat up. She started to scream, thin childish screams of sheer horror. She scrambled to her feet, wailing, 'Stop it, stop it, oh let the poor thing go. Oh please please please –' She was up against the wall, as if she was trying to fight her way through it. I could see the grey metal through her transparent hands. 'Don't do it, don't do it, oh no no oh poor pussy, no please don't hurt him more –' sobbed the little ghost.

Dittany adjusted something. I could see black boxes on

the tabletop: but couldn't see what she was doing to them. The terrified child flickered, like a three-dimensional video running backwards: and then forwards. She was crouching on the floor again, whimpering and pleading.

'Tell us what's wrong,' begged Dittany, her hoarse voice full of concern now.

'Oh please, stop them from taking me away –'

Another flicker. 'Don't let them take poor Stacey away! They'll take me where you cannot find me. *Oh please, please, please.*'

The same weeping, the same movements, the same struggling to speak through terrified sobs: but the words were different. 'They know you're trying to get me. They're going to hurt me more and more. Oh please don't let them hurt me more!'

I wouldn't have been able to spot what was going on, except that they kept on re-running the same sequences until I could see for myself the tiny slips, the places where the girl's lip movements didn't fit the soundtrack in the remixed version . . . Dittany, and the person out of sight, discussed in low voices the perfect match that was their goal.

I realized that I knew how they had used that foul hologram clip of the cat being killed.

They'd used it to frighten the little girl who was supposed to be Stacey. They'd used it to make her fear seem utterly real. Now they were editing a recording of how the child had reacted, and giving her a different script.

I understood that this new movie, when they'd finished it, would be shown to my mother. She would see her baby terrified and pleading for mercy. She would be told that this was happening far away. Dittany and Doric would be as bewildered and helpless, supposedly, as Mum herself. They had lured her into their clutches with the messages, and then images of a little girl who genuinely seemed to be Stacey. Now it was time for the sting. It was classic.

You have to co-operate, they would say. You have to do exactly what we tell you, or we cannot rescue your daughter from this awful fate.

Whatever it was –

But what did they want from Mum? It couldn't be money. *We didn't have this kind of money!* We couldn't possibly raise the kind of ransom (because that was what it was) that would make all this expensive future-tech trickery worthwhile. The NIMROD people knew everything. They must know about the poor financial situation of the Robarts family, even if you took into account Jo Brennan and his police-executive salary.

If it wasn't money, *what did they want from us?*

'Now come over here, you naughty girl. Come to Mum.'

I'd missed something. They'd started to work on a different recording, 'Stacey' in a different mood again. She wasn't crying in this one. She came towards the table, slowly and reluctantly. In the two NIMROD sessions I had seen, 'Stacey' had not looked at anyone, she'd seemed unaware of anybody in the room. She was 'in the grey place', where she could hear Dittany's questions but couldn't see any of us. This child stared angrily, directly at the spot where Dittany was standing. A defiant, miserable scowl twisted her little mouth.

'Stand up straight.'

She stood straight, chin trembling, her eyes blazing fury.

'Say after me: My name is Stacey Robarts. Hepup, hepup me, I am frightened.'

'My name is Stacey Robarts. Help, help –'

'Hepup, hepup.'

The child grimaced. 'That's *stupid*, I don't say that any more, I'm not a baby.'

'I am very frightened, please do whatever they say, to stop them from hurting me.'

She shook her head violently. 'I'm NEVER frighte-ned.'

I knew I was watching some kind of recording. But the impression that the transparent little figure was really there, staring at Dittany and answering her, was hard to resist. I started to have a strange and horrible thought. Supposing there was no living child, still hidden some-where. Suppose that really was my sister's ghost? She looked like Stacey, she behaved like Stacey . . . Older, different: do the dead grow older? Maybe they do, if they are held captive by some malign power.

I'd always been scared of Dittany. I hated her hooded eyes and her silver claws, her spooky false goodwill. What if she genuinely did have some kind of evil psychic abilities? What if Demetria and I were both right? The NIMROD gang had my sister in their power, *but Stacey was still dead . . . ?*

I wanted to jump up and yell. Leap over the partition, thump Dittany, grab the kid and run for it. Anything to shatter the atmosphere in that next room. But how do you grab a ghost, and where would I run?

'Repeat after me. Please do whatever they ask you to do. I want to come home.'

'Please do whatever they ask . . . It's not true, I don't HAVE A HOME!'

But she couldn't keep it up. She crouched down, head in her hands. 'Go away go away go away,' she sobbed. 'Oh go away, leave me alone, go away –'

'Okay,' said someone. 'Stop it there. We'll remix that footage later.'

The small ghost flickered into nothingness. Dittany pulled a headset of black wire out of her bird's-nest hairdo. 'Oh yes, you do have a home, little girl,' she said. She patted one of the black boxes, with satisfaction. 'It's in here.'

'Looking good.' The voice was a man's. A hand came into my view, a man's hand holding a cigar: stubby-fingered and wearing a gold ring. 'I think Mrs Robarts is going to find the next session very persuasive.'

The person the hand belonged to leaned forward. Of course it was Doric, the dapper Mr Kaplan. He knocked off the ash from his cigar against the edge of the black box. After what Dittany had said, it was as if he was dropping ash on that crying child. I could imagine him doing that. 'You get wonderful performances out of our child star, obstinate little tyke that she is. You're doing a very fine job.'

'It's the material you give me, Mr Kaplan,' simpered the old witch (if a toad can simper). 'You're so intelligent. The pussycat works on her wonderfully, better than it does on the adults. It's not so much that the cat dies. She's a tough little ragamuffin. It's the way it comes back to life, and she knows we will kill it again. That's a lovely stroke.'

'As long as it works,' said Mr Kaplan smugly. I wished I could punch him. How I despised these two slimy jerks. 'Okay, let's go. We'll use this as our studio until the wrap, now. No one is to go back to the flat, it's not worth the risk. High tide at dawn. When they've unloaded our cargo they'll take off the boy and dump him in the channel somewhere.'

'Shall we check on him now?' I barely caught the words, they were muttered very softly. So there was a *third* person in there –

I froze. I didn't dare to move, not even to pull the matting over my head.

'No.' Mr Kaplan sounded offended at the suggestion. 'Not while I'm here. He's asleep, or out cold. Leave him alone. You disturb him now, he might have to be restrained and I don't want a mark on him. If he's awake in the morning it'll be okay. You can tell him another story, to get him to go on board quietly. After that it's not going to matter what he knows.'

So I was saved from a dangerous moment, because Mr

Kaplan wasn't the sort to get his hands dirty. The footsteps receded. I waited for a long time before I dared to move.

I stumbled out on to the dock. My head was throbbing like crazy. How was I going to get out of here? Did that blank barrier at the seaward end seal the cave completely? Maybe I could swim underneath it. But deep water scared me, and since the day that Stacey vanished I'd done no swimming at all, couldn't stand the idea. I couldn't see myself escaping that way. The effort of staggering out of the locker room had made my head swim and brought a foul taste to my mouth. I dropped to my knees with my head over the side. When I'd chucked up everything I'd eaten for the last week – that's how it felt – I rolled over on my back. The water made its faint slop-slopping noises. But what was that other sound, that mouse-like scratching and tapping, lost in the echoes?

I sat up, carefully. Someone was in here with me . . .

The 'changing rooms' were empty. I looked into them one by one. They reminded me of the cellars under The Casbah restaurant: all these hooks, all these lockers, as if the place was equipped for a crowd of people. What had happened to them all? I saved the section where Dittany had been working on the recordings until last. It was as empty as the others, except for the table, three metal chairs and the smell of cigar smoke.

'Stacey?' I whispered.

Again, that tapping sound . . .

Then I saw something lying on the floor, in the corner by the door: as if someone had kicked it there in passing. I bent to see what it was, and found a small black box. I knelt down to have a closer look. I had seen this particular futuristic toy before.

It was Demetria's electronic lockpick.

She'd told me that she'd infiltrated NIMROD. She must have been the third person in this room just now, whose voice I had barely heard. She knew I'd been captured and she'd managed to leave the lockpick behind for me. I grabbed it, grinning in relief, before realizing that I'd made another of my leaps in the dark. But I seemed to have got away with it. The lockpick was not booby-trapped. It didn't blow up, or start ticking.

If she'd left this behind to help me escape, there had to be an exit from this cavern besides the sea door. I must be able to find it, and use this thing on the lock. I tried to reconstruct my memory. I'd been on a boat after I was knocked out, but I didn't think I'd been brought here by sea. There had been a journey in a car or a van, there had been a bumpy descent, like being let down a well –

The tapping had either begun again or it had never stopped. It suddenly grew louder. And now, as I held my breath and listened, I could hear something more. Someone was faintly calling.

'*Help, help, I'm trapped in a fortune factory!*'

The hairs stood up at the back of my neck.

'Stacey?' I called, hoarsely.

'*Help, help!*'

'Stacey? Where are you?'

'*My name is Stacey Robarts, I'm trapped in a fortune factory!*'

'Chinese fortune cookie factory,' I muttered, automatically. She could never get that punch line right. I couldn't tell where the voice was coming from. 'Stacey, *where are you?*'

I stumbled out into the main cave. There was some kind of engine house at the end of the dock. The dark water rocked in its deep pen. *I'm buried under the sea defences, the fishes have eaten me . . .* 'Keep calling!' I shouted, trying to steady my voice. 'I'll find you!'

But I was sick and battered and overwrought. I was afraid I would find the original of NIMROD's ghost-child, and it would be my sister Stacey, three years dead. I thought of my mother, her arms stretched out with longing to the image we'd been shown. What would the real Stacey look like by now? If they had found her, if she had been washed in here. If Mr Kaplan had used his astonishing gadgets to steal the memories from a dead child's brain. A brain in a jar, wires trailing. A little girl smashed to pieces on the rocks, pulled back into shape by ugly magic. Locked up in this grey place and whispering to the electrodes planted in her skull: about Mum and Dad and Alan, a cat called Bono and a house with a red front door . . .

When you know that you have been responsible for a child's death: when you know you are guilty, no matter what anyone says, then your mind becomes open to horrors. You will believe whatever seems bad enough to be true.

I found a rough walled corridor beyond the locker rooms, and then another room, bigger and more solid, with a bolted-down table and chairs, bunks and a cooker. There was a bathroom at the end. The grey walls sighed at me, the whole cavern was a whispering galley, a nest of echoes. '*Help help . . . fortune factory . . . my name is Stacey . . .*'

I called her name, dreading that she would answer, afraid to find her, desperate to know –

The whispering had stopped. But I knew she was there, close to me now. Stacey loved playing hide-and-seek.

'Well,' I said loudly. 'Looks like she isn't in here. I think I'm going to give up.'

'*Getting warmer! Getting warmer!*'

It was a child's clear voice, not an echo.

Three raps, from the wall beside me.

I studied the place where the rapping had come from. It was in the space between two sets of bunks. There was a panel standing out from the wall, about a metre square with a grid of small holes in the middle, like an air vent. It seemed to be held in place by four wing nuts, which looked shiny as if from frequent twisting. They moved easily. The panel came free, I hauled it clear and chucked

—— 113 ——

it aside. Something scuffed, like an animal. Two bright, hard eyes stared at me. A small hand came up, brandishing a gleaming, sharp-edged strip of metal.

Then the fierce expression on the child's face changed to beaming joy.

'My Alan!'

She leapt out into my arms.

I dropped her in shock. She jumped to her feet. No ghost, but a living breathing girl in a shabby tracksuit. 'I knew it!' she beamed, dancing up and down. 'My Alan! I knew you would come! I knew it was you!'

I gently took the weapon from her hand. She didn't resist. It was a sort of home-made knife: a sliver of sharpened metal, one end bound in rags.

'So what was *this* for?'

She grinned proudly. 'That's my shiv. They don't know I've got it. I made it myself. You can keep it for now,' she offered. 'But you'll have to give it back if they attack us. You see, I heard them talking. I knew they'd brought my Alan here, so when they'd gone, I called to you. But I wasn't *completely* sure it was you, so I kept the shiv ready. But it *is* you, and you're *here*!'

I looked inside the opening. I saw a tiny cell, painted grey, with a little bunk and a dim fluorescent tube for lighting. 'Do they *keep* you in there?' I demanded.

'Often they do. When I've been bad they keep me in my cell for days. Sometimes I'm very bad.' She bared her teeth. 'I try to *kill* anyone who comes near me. But not with my shiv, because then they'd take it away, and I want to save it for killing *her*.'

I could bet I knew who *her* was. The hideous Dittany.

'How did you know my name?'

'Because I have your picture, of course.' She pointed. Inside the cell, taped up on that mousehole wall, were recent photographs of me, and Mum, and the house with the red door. 'I knew that they were showing the movies of me to Alan and Mum. I couldn't see you, but I knew you would see me. So I called: *Hepup, hepup, I'm being held prisoner in a fortune factory.* I *knew* you'd remember. You're my Alan, and I'm your little sister Stacey. I dreamed and dreamed that you would come to save me!'

I was still feeling sick with relief, because reality had been restored. The 'living ghost' was a child who looked like Stacey, an ordinary little imposter: just the explanation I'd always thought most likely. 'Yeah,' I said. 'I remember what my little sister used to say. But you're not my sister. That's their con-trick. My sister's dead.'

I was ashamed of having been so spooked. I didn't think how cruel I was being.

She stared at me for a long moment.

'I was afraid I probably wasn't,' she said at last, with a sad little nod. I hadn't ever noticed it before, but I could hear the slight foreign accent now. 'But I hoped I might be, because I don't remember being anyone else.' She shrugged her shoulders, and her stubborn little chin came up. 'Oh well, I suppose I must be some other lost little girl.'

'I'm sorry.'

I don't know how a normal child would have reacted. But this was not a normal child. How could she be, after the way she'd been treated?

'It doesn't matter. You can still be my Alan. Will you rescue me anyway?'

'Yeah. I'll rescue you.' I didn't know how I was going to rescue either of us, but I had Demetria's lockpick, and I'd think of something. 'But you have to tell me what's going on. Tell me who you really are. And why have you been pretending to be my sister?'

'I haven't been *pretending*. I hoped it was true.' 'Stacey' walked past me and sat at the table that ran down the middle of the room, propped her elbows on it and set her chin in her hands. 'If I'm not your sister,' she went on, 'then I don't know *who* I am. I don't properly remember anywhere but here. I think I've lost my memories. The only thing I remember is that *she* taught me to be Stacey. I've learnt so many things off by heart, things Stacey knew and things she would say. I was *hoping* it might really be true.' Her wistful expression changed to a ferocious scowl. 'But I know one thing. SHE is not my mother! I HATE HATE HATE it when she says *come to Mother!*'

'Does she hurt you?'

'No one hurts *me*. Not even when I hit them and kick them and bite them. *She* used to tell me she would hurt me, but I wasn't scared. So now she says she will hurt the poor cat again, if I don't behave. Or she says she will throw Torquil away, and I will never get him back.'

'*What* did you say?'

She bit her lip. Tears had come into her eyes. 'I know the cat thing is a movie. I'm not a baby. I know the scary things in movies are not real . . . It makes me cry every time, but I've promised myself the poor cat is alive somewhere, and they haven't really hurt him. But *she took Torquil*.' She dug in the pocket of her tracksuit trousers and brought out a small purple plastic case. 'She took his insides and his batteries. She says she'll throw them away, and he'll be dead.'

Torquil.

My heart began to thump wildly. It couldn't be. This must be another cyberpet toy, that looked like the one my sister had with her when she vanished, the one that had never been found. My mouth was dry.

'Do you have anything else,' I croaked. 'Anything else, that used to belong to Stacey?'

'Torquil's *mine*. And you said I wasn't Stacey.'

'Could I have a closer look?'

She stuffed the empty case back in her pocket. 'No!'

I felt as if something had shaken loose inside me. Some barrier had fallen, and all the secret hope I'd been feeling, since Demetria first told me Stacey was alive, suddenly came pouring through. There was no ghost, there was a living girl. *What if she wasn't an imposter?*

Older ... different ... spirited away by NIMROD three years ago, and now just as mysteriously returned. If she had forgotten her past, and they had taught her to remember it again, wouldn't Stacey be just like this? Little tough nut, scared of nothing. Except losing her only treasure, the one thing she had left to love ...

Just because the bad guys want you to believe something, that doesn't mean it isn't true.

'H-how long?' I stammered. 'How long have you been here? Where did you live before?'

She heaved a theatrical sigh. 'Well, I don't know that, do I? It's a few weeks or a few months, or a few years. I'm not sure which. I don't know where I was before. I told you: I've lost my memories. It's no use asking me because I *don't remember*.' She hopped down from her chair. 'Now we'd better hurry up. The heavies will be here soon, to get ready for the cargo. I know when a cargo is coming, because *she* gives me the stinky cocoa. It's to make me go to sleep, but I pour it down my toilet. She puts lots of sugar in to hide the taste, but I know: and I stay awake and hear things.'

'Wait a minute. What *is* the cargo, anyway? What's going on? What's this place for?'

'You mean you don't know?'

'Call me Mr Pitiful. I don't know anything. So tell.'

Her thin little face took on a ridiculously superior expression. 'Well, Mr Pitiful, I'm not supposed to know either, but I do. It's aliens. Aliens from outer space. Mr Kaplan is helping them invade the earth. I think –' She pressed her two index fingers on either side of her nose. 'I *think* they must have given him, Mr Kaplan – Doric is his NIMROD name – his special cameras and laser beams, because I've heard Davros say his gear is out of this world.'

'Who's Davros?'

'One of the aliens. He was here before, he helped them bring you, I think. The heavies are the ones that keep us humans under control. They're disguised as humans so they can go around with Mr Kaplan and make sure he doesn't do a double-cross. The aliens have paid him to help them invade earth, you see.'

Aliens from outer space. Oh, I wished she hadn't said that.

It was something that had crossed my mind. Not that I'd seriously thought it could be true: but I could see where Demetria's dark hints of an incredible conspiracy might be heading. Oh no, I thought. Please God, no. Give me some explanation that makes *sense* . . . She gazed at me innocently. That was Stacey all over. She'd tell you the most incredible whoppers without turning a hair. Then when you'd gently try to tell her she was imagining things, she'd roar with laughter. Maybe she was teasing me now.

'Come off it, Stace. There's no such thing as aliens from outer space.'

'But there are! I've *seen* them! Lots of them. They're fairly like humans, only most of them are thinner, and they have funny voices, and they have to be disguised in special clothes –' She glared at me, but then her eyes widened. 'You called me Stace! So now do you think I *am* your sister?'

My head, which was throbbing as if there was a steam engine inside my skull, had started to spin. 'Let's stop this. We'll discuss the aliens and the invasion and your secret identity another time. Let's concentrate on our escape.'

She genuinely didn't know of any exit except by sea. She had no idea, as far as I could make out, where in the world she was. It could actually have been an alien planet out there, and she wouldn't have known any different. We took one of the torches that were hanging on the wall and explored to the end of the corridor, beyond the room where she'd been kept prisoner. Just before the light from the bulkhead lamps gave out completely, the torch beam found a break in the passage floor. There was a seawater smell and a rushing, gurgling sound: water surged, down in the dark. But beyond the break, which was quite narrow, I could see the hasps of an iron ladder, driven into rock, disappearing up into the dark.

'I can't swim,' said Stacey worriedly.

This was the way I'd been brought in. I was sure of it.

'No, but you can climb. I'm going to jump across, holding you, and we're going up there.'

'Okay, Alan. If you say so.'

She looked up at me, smiling, full of cheerful courage in the torchlight. My memory did a back flip, something like the thing they call *déjà vu*. Surely I'd had this same conversation before, with this same brave, punchy little kid. On a summer's day in bright sunlight, halfway up the chalk cliffs, between the blue sea and the sky . . .

I had been ready to believe back in the cavern. Now I was completely sure. We were trapped in the dark, but I was flying in a clear sky. She *was* my sister.

There was a lump in my throat. I stooped down and hugged her hard.

'That's my girl. We can do it.'

Then, I had an idea. 'Just a minute. There's something I want to try –'

I hustled her back down the corridor and on to the dock, protesting all the way. 'We shouldn't go back! My Alan, don't be crazy, they'll be here soon –'

'Shush, I know what I'm doing.'

The engine house at the end of the dock was locked: and yes, it was an electronic lock. Nothing but high tech for Mr Kaplan. I studied the tiny controls on Demetria's gadget, trying to remember what I'd seen her do with it: and then applied my instant expertise. There was a button you could press that brought up the liquid crystal display: SCRAMBLE.

'What are you doing? We ought to be getting away! If they catch us they'll kill you!'

'I'm not sure. But it's possible that I've locked your heavies out of the works. They won't be able to open the sea door when their cargo ship wants to come in.'

She beamed. 'The aliens won't like that!' Her eyes sparkled. 'Maybe they'll kill Mr Kaplan. Maybe they'll kill *Dittany*! Maybe they'll make her head burst. That would be great!'

'Yeah, wouldn't it. C'mon kiddo. Let's get out of here!'

Back to the other exit. I swung her over the rushing channel, and we climbed. At the top of the ladder there was a platform and a door. The door was old iron, with corrosion under the new grey paint. But it had been modernized. I applied Demetria's box of tricks to the electronic lock. After a couple of mystic passes ... something clicked.

Stacey was impressed.

'Where did you get that thing of yours?' she asked. 'That's an *aliens*' thing.'

'No, it isn't. It's a normal dodgy gizmo, you can buy them anywhere.' I'd never actually seen an electronic lockpick in Maplins, but I was sure this was right. 'Demetria left it for us. You know Demetria, don't you? The pretty one, with the blonde hair?'

She frowned. 'Yes, I know that one. But –'

'She's secretly on our side. She was with them when the bad guys brought me here, and she managed to leave this for me to find.'

'*Demetria?*' said Stacey, doubtfully. 'Are you sure?'

'Yeah, well, I don't think it was Doric or your friend Dittany that kindly left us a key.'

The door was stiff, it scraped over the ground: but it opened.

We were in one of the old pillboxes on the top of Beachcombe cliffs: a brick-built gun-emplacement left over from the Second World War. It was a dark and dirty little hovel and it smelt of wee, but I felt like kissing the ground. Outside, the sky was pale. I looked at my watch. It was four thirty in the morning. There was a breeze from the sea, and it was cold.

'What are we going to do now?' asked Stacey.

She was staring around her with a strange expression, as if she was trying to recall the meaning of these things: sea, sky, fresh air, grass and flowers. I wondered how long it was since she'd seen the outside world. I thought about ways that we could prove she was Stacey: DNA testing, something like that. I reminded myself (though really it was too late, I'd given them up already) that I must wait until all the questions were answered, before I let go of my last doubts. But where could I take her right now? I couldn't take her home, that was the first place NIM-ROD would come looking. I didn't feel like going to Beachcombe police station with a story about aliens from outer space.

'We'd better get away from here quickly,' I said. 'You can stay with a friend of mine, someone I can trust, until we've sorted everything.'

It was six by the time we reached Mo's. We had to walk, because there were no buses about. Mo was great, as I'd known he would be. He was already up. He didn't sleep much. He'd told me he usually spent the night reading. He let us in, got Stacey a blanket to wrap round her because her teeth were chattering, and started making us breakfast, before he asked any questions at all. The smell of frying bacon made me realize I was starving. So was Stacey. I don't know what they'd fed her on in that secret den, but she sat on Mo's bed, with a mug of navvy-strong sweet tea in one hand, and an enormous doorstep bacon sandwich in the other, tucking in as if she hadn't eaten for a month.

I tried to explain to Mo who she was and where she came from. As much as I knew. When I described a secret cavern under the cliffs, I didn't think he'd believe me. But trust Mo. He knew all about it . . . or at least, about what kind of place it was.

'Oh yes. Sounds like a submarine pen. That'd be one of the stay-behind places.'

'What's one of those?'

'It was in the Second World War. When they thought the Nazis were going to invade, they made preparations for the resistance. All along this coast there's tunnels and caves and secret harbours, hidden from the outside, meant to be used by what they called the stay-behinds. I never heard of a cave like that between Beachcombe and Seastead but I'm not surprised. A lot of those wartime things were abandoned and forgotten. It could be there, and no one know about it –'

'The aliens have hidden the entrance,' Stacey piped up. 'They can do anything.'

'Aliens?' repeated Mo.

'Aliens from outer space,' I explained. 'According to Stacey, that's what's behind all this. The NIMROD gang is cover for an alien invasion. Somehow, the invasion plans involve my mum. That's why they claimed they could get Stacey back, so they could blackmail her into doing their bidding –' I laughed, to show I knew this was ridiculous.

It was fascinating to watch how Mo managed the breakfast things. He hadn't let me help him, he preferred to do everything himself. He'd fried the bacon and buttered the bread and made the tea one-handed, shifting neatly about in his kitchenette so his unreliable left side couldn't mess things up. He paused now, in the middle of pouring me a second mug of tea; put the pot down and scratched his nose with his good right hand.

'Well, I dunno why you're laughing. They've got to turn up sometime, haven't they?'

'Leave it out, Mo. Aliens from outer space!'

'It's a big old galaxy, we can't be all alone. And *when* they turn up, hardly no one's going to believe it at first.

—— 122 ——

Stands to reason. It's been done so often on the telly and in the movies, it can't be true. That's what people will think.'

'But Mo, you don't seriously believe –'

'All I'm saying is, it has to happen some time. What I really want to know is what are you going to do with this little girl? It's Sunday. You and me, we have to be at work by nine. Who's going to look after her?'

I'd forgotten about Countryfare: but that was a problem easily solved.

'I won't go in. Could I stay here with her? Just for today, until I work something out –'

Mo looked glum. It dawned on me that I was doing my leap-before-you-look thing again. He lived alone, he was disabled. I'd just told him I was mixed up with something that involved criminals who were prepared to commit murder. From Mo's point of view, it didn't make much difference whether the bad guys were monsters from outer space or the Russian Mafia. I was still asking him to risk his neck.

The entryphone rang.

Mo and I looked at each other. He limped across the room and listened to it. 'It's your friend Caz,' he said. 'I suppose it's all right for her to know about the little girl?' He jerked his head at 'Stacey', who had finished her sandwich and was licking brown sauce and bacon grease from her fingers.

'Oh, yeah. Caz is okay.' Though I couldn't imagine what she was doing here.

'But I've got to get to the store. I'll tell 'em you're sick, shall I?'

Caz knocked on the door. I went out into Mo's tiny front hall to open it. When she saw me, an enormous smile burst over her features. 'Alan! You're okay!'

'What are you doing here?'

'I want to know what happened! I stayed by the phone,

like you said, till late: but you didn't call. So I called your house. Your mum answered, and she was getting worried. So I said you'd been with me, but you'd gone off with some friends, and I was supposed to tell her you were going fishing and you might not get back all night.'

I was so used to our routine, I'd completely forgotten that Mum was at our house, not round at Jo Brennan's, as she ought to have been this weekend. 'What did you do that for?' I demanded, unfairly. 'I didn't ask you to tell my mum anything. Why d'you have to say *fishing*? I don't even own a fishing rod –'

'I dunno, it just came to me. So this morning I came here, because I didn't know where else you might be. Come on, Al. I saved your skin, don't yell at me.'

'Oh, all right. Come in. And thanks for saving my skin.'

She took a step into the hall, and then jumped back with a grin. 'Whoops, I forgot the password!' She began to wave her hands.

I might have known she'd been watching, outside The Casbah. She was trying to do the NIMROD signs. I groaned. 'Trust you. You're doing it all wrong. Look, it goes like this –'

Mo had come out to see what was happening. He looked at us, and his face changed.

'What's that with the hand-jive, Al?'

'You mean this?' I did the signs again. He nodded, and turned away.

Caz and I followed him back into his room.

'Caz, this is "Stacey". I mean, this is the kid NIM-ROD were keeping hostage. They've been showing videos of her to my mum, claiming they'd found my little sister. But I rescued her –'

'Is that what you were doing last night? Hey, cool. Tell me all about it!'

But I was distracted. Mo had returned to his chair, and was twisting himself up there, in his spider pose. He had looked glum before. Now he looked a lot worse. As if suddenly the whole adventure had become deadly –

'*Mo?* What's up?'

'I've seen that hand-jive,' he admitted. 'And I don't like it . . . I don't like this at all, Al.'

'What did he say?' demanded Caz, rudely.

'He's recognized the NIMROD signs,' I translated. 'He knows something.'

'I don't know much,' said Mo. 'But I've heard things . . . You don't want to cross those hand-jive people. They're big-time nasty. They'll do you in, for nothing. That's what I've heard.'

'But who *are* they, Mo?'

'I don't know. If you've got any sense you stay out of their business, that's all.'

'He's right,' cried 'Stacey', who seemed to have no trouble understanding Mo. Her face was suddenly pinched with fear. 'You shouldn't have rescued me, Alan. The aliens will kill you. They'll kill us all, and they'll make us disappear –'

'Don't *say* that,' I shouted, much louder than I meant. 'They can't possibly be *aliens!*'

I was seeing visions of those cellars, the store of shabby clothes, the heaps of camping mattresses. People Mo Doyle knew weren't likely to be using the Internet. They would be living on the margins, selling *The Big Issue*, queuing up at the DSS, taking dead-end casual work. The kind of people who would not be missed. Maybe it made sense, a horrible kind of sense. Stolen lives, the bodies somehow disposed of, the clothes and the identities handed out to NIMROD's weird customers, so they could blend into the human world.

We stared at each other, me and Mo and Caz. It seemed to me that all three of us were thinking the impossible, thinking *it could be true*. This could be it. *They* could be here . . .

There was another knock on the door. None of us

noticed that we hadn't heard the entryphone. Caz went to open it. I heard a man's voice, calm and official-sounding, say: 'We'd like to speak to Mr Alan Robarts, if he's here.'

They came into the room, two big broad men in suits. I knew who they were the moment I saw them, but I was paralysed with dismay –

Mo stood up. He managed to do it so clumsily he knocked over the armchair. Trust Mo, he kept his eye on the ball. But it was too late, it was no good. They brushed him aside as if he was made of matchsticks. One of the men leaned over, took 'Stacey' by the arm and lifted her clear into the air. She started to scream and fight. But Mo was down, he couldn't get up. The second man easily blocked Caz and me while the first man swept the child out of the door. He took a cold look round the room, like he was committing its contents to memory for later attention, and he was gone too.

Caz and I ran down the stairs, Mo limping after us. We were shouting, because what other weapon did we have? We shouted, 'Stop! Stop them! They're taking that little girl! They're kidnapping her! Stop them!'

But it was early on a Sunday morning, and nobody in the building stirred.

In the street, they were bundling her into a dark-coloured car. She was fighting them, and screaming like mad at the top of her voice. There was no one in sight, not a curtain twitched. One of the men was in the driver's seat, the other had thrown 'Stacey' into the back and got in beside her. I grabbed on to the handle of the car door. But the car took off, and I had to let go. I was kneeling in the road, sobbing with horror and frustrated rage . . .

I had lost her again.

*She was right beside me, Mum. I couldn't help it. I couldn't do anything. A man in a car grabbed her and took her away . . .*

'Call the coppers,' gasped Mo. 'Quick. Tell them everything you know.'

'No!'

'Alan, we have to call the police –' wailed Caz.

'NO! I can't! I can't risk it. *They've got "Stacey".*'

The three of us went back up the stairs. Mo's door was open, the armchair was still on the floor. The cockatiels were whistling on the next-door balcony.

'How did they know where we were?' I moaned. 'How did they know to come here?'

Mo's room was spinning. Everything looked sinister and fake and full of secrets: the strange assortment of plates and mugs, the shabby furniture, the boxes of second-hand books. Everything in the world was suddenly false, there was no one I could believe in.

'It was me,' burst out Caz. They must have followed me! They saw me with you last night, and they must have followed me this morning. Oh, Alan, I'm sorry! We've got to tell my dad!'

'*You got to call the police*,' insisted Mo. 'Those are bad lads, Alan. You don't know what they might do to a little girl.'

Well, they tried, but I wouldn't be moved. I knew there was only one person who could help me now. It had to be Demetria.

# *Eleven*

*I* TOLD CAZ TO GO HOME, BEHAVE NORMALLY, AND not say a word to anyone about what had happened. Least of all to her dad. Then I called my mum. I had to back up Caz's ridiculous story about the fishing expedition, and stop her from worrying. Or so I thought. But Mum wasn't very interested in me or my whereabouts. She'd had a call from Dittany, at last. There was going to be another session. The old witch had warned her that there were unexpected developments, and what she saw this time 'might be distressing'. Mum couldn't talk about anything else.

'I can't believe it, we were so close. I keep trying to get on to the website, but I can't get through. Too much traffic on the web, or something.'

She was obviously making an effort to keep calm, but her voice sounded panicky. I thought of the little ghost I'd seen in that locker room, crying and pleading. It was unbearable to know that thanks to me 'Stacey' was back there: in the grey place. That it was my fault, again. I didn't know what to say.

'Look, I'm at Mo Doyle's. I stopped off to – er – clean up after the fishing. I'm going straight to work. Will you be home this evening, or are you going round to Jo's?'

A silence at the other end of the line. 'I'm not going round,' she said at last. 'See you later.'

She hung up. The lobby of Mo's building, battered and drab, looked like a prison or a long-term hospital. A place without hope. I felt sick. I couldn't stand the thought of telling my mother what had happened. If I had lost Stacey again, I simply could not go home. I would not go home. I would walk away, with the clothes on my back and whatever money I happened to have in my pockets, and never return. This is how you become a missing person, I thought. When your life is so ruined there's no way you can carry on living it. This is how it feels.

I went to work instead.

I had no means of contacting Demetria: no phone number, no address, no information at all. It was too late to kick myself for not insisting on a little less mystery. But it didn't matter. I knew that she would contact me. She would turn up in the supermarket, the way she did the first time. I was certain of it. I had to be certain, because I had no other hope.

I crawled through that Sunday. Everybody except Mo thought I had a killer hangover. So on top of my pounding head, and my terror and remorse and dread, I had to cope with the good-natured 'teasing' of my workmates. Even Big Liz decided to put in her contribution, taking me aside and giving me a serious warning against underage drinking.

I couldn't stop myself from re-running that scene in my head. The lie that had become the truth this time round, like a punishment from a wicked god. The little girl, screaming. The little girl fighting like a tiger, that big, gloved hand fastened on her like some kind of monstrous insect. The man throwing her into the car. She is still fighting as it drives away, and I'm kneeling in the road . . .

There was still something very wrong between Mum and Jo. I was afraid it must be something to do with the NIMROD business. Jo must have stopped thinking NIMROD was the cure for our troubles, long ago. He called, several times. She wouldn't talk to him. Once I heard her telling him to get off the line, because she was waiting for a call from Dittany. She spoke coldly as if she was talking to a stranger. I didn't dare ask what was going on. Between the two of us, it was back to the bad old days. On Monday morning she came into the kitchen while I was trying to eat breakfast, made herself a cup of tea: drank it, left, and shut herself in the Stacey Operations Centre, all without even looking at me.

I went to the store, put on my green coat and started work. As soon as Mo saw me he came over. 'Al, you can't carry on like this. You gotta go to the police. You don't know what you're getting yourself into. Think of that little girl –'

I walked away. I wasn't going to try and explain myself. There was no way he could possibly understand what I had to do.

She turned up about midday. I had been watching the entrance and scanning the aisles, but I didn't see her until she was next to me, looking at fancy preserves: in the same aisle where I was unloading kilo bags of sugar. She wasn't wearing the baseball cap or the sunglasses, or the silver earrings; but she was dressed in white shorts and a white T-shirt that showed off her sporty figure. She gave me one glance. I pushed my pallet closer, close enough to count the feathers of blonde hair that curled on the nape of her neck.

'Queen Victoria,' she said quietly. 'When you get off work. Six o'clock. Remember?'

The summer, that had started out so generous with its sunshine and flowers, had begun to fade. It was the season of dull bedding plants in municipal gardens, dusty skies, and trees that looked tired of being green. The sun was shining, but there was a strengthening wind that blew the litter about and threw grit into people's eyes. There was a bus stop outside the Queen Victoria: that's what made it a good place to wait without being noticeable. At six o'clock, Demetria was there. When she saw me coming she took off, walking briskly towards the town centre and the sea. I followed. In the park by the bus station she sat down on a bench. There were people practising unseasonable football on the grass. There were kids on skateboards and bicycles, little children with their mums and dads in the playground. She'd put on her sunglasses, and taken a magazine out of her shoulder bag. She put it away as I sat down beside her.

'Hello, Alan,' she said.

I was glad we weren't going to pretend not to know each other, talking out of the sides of our mouths like comic-book secret agents. I wasn't in the mood for games.

'You know what happened?'

'I know that you went back to Kaplan's flat,' she told me. 'You were caught, and they took you to the Arrivals Hall. I did what I could to help.'

'Arrivals Hall? Why do you call it that?'

'It's not the moment to explain.' The dark lenses hid her eyes, but her mouth was ruefully smiling. 'You found the Grand Hotel too, didn't you? I should have known you'd go after NIMROD on your own . . . Well, they took "Stacey" back. What are we going to do now?'

'It was the *Diamond Life*,' I said. 'That's why you were on the sea defences, three years ago. You were watching for the *Diamond Life*. You had a phone with you. Who were you going to call? Was it Davros, or one of the other heavies? To tell them to open the sea door.'

'What are you talking about? It's true, I was watching for the *Diamond Life*. But I'm not –'

'One of the bad guys? I'm not so sure. I've been thinking about a few things. Like that gadget of yours,' I went on. 'It isn't a lockpick. It's simply a key, with your usual combinations entered in the memory. Like Kaplan's flat, like the back door of that place under the cliffs. You seem to have infiltrated NIMROD very successfully. You're like one of the family.'

'Alan, it isn't what you think –'

Suddenly I knew something else, something that should have been blindingly obvious from the beginning. '*You* took Stacey! It must have been you. You were there. While I was gone, she saw something suspicious, I don't know what, and *you kidnapped her*. There must be another way into the cavern, near that path up to the clifftop. You took her, into that place you call the Arrivals Hall.'

For a moment she was silent, staring ahead of her. Then she said, 'Alan, I swear to you: I *didn't* kidnap your sister . . . But you're right. I have been working in deep cover, for quite a while. I'm sorry. I should have told you more. But I couldn't take the risk. It's important that the NIMROD people go on accepting me as one of themselves. When you were caught I had to protect myself. I left my unilock behind for you. I hoped you and "Stacey" would get right away. But you didn't. What matters now is that you *have to do exactly as I say*, if you want to see her again.'

I wished I knew what was going on behind those glasses.

'What do you want me to do?'

'I want you to take a document folder from the filing cabinet in Joachim Brennan's study, and bring it to me at the Marina.'

I had been doing a lot of thinking since I lost Stacey for a second time. I'd come to some tough conclusions. But this amazed me.

'Jo!' I exclaimed. '*Jo Brennan?* What has Jo got to do with it!'

'Everything. I believe he's in their pay.'

'What do you mean? Whose pay?'

'You remember I said, people who get near to what's going on behind NIMROD disappear? Or else they change their minds, and decide there is nothing to investigate? Jo Brennan is one of those. Something that turned up in one of his fraud cases led him to NIMROD. He was collecting evidence against them, but then he stopped. I think he's taking their money. He's been trying

to sabotage my investigation, and he has removed a
certain file from police records. But he's been hanging on
to the material, he hasn't destroyed it yet. It's in that
folder. You have to burgle his study for me, if you dare,
and get it back. I think I can fix up a trade. The file on
NIMROD, for your sister.'

*If you dare,* she said. I remembered the night we'd
broken into Doric's penthouse. But I wasn't going to be
tempted by the thrill of risk and danger.

'I don't get it, Demetria. If this file's so important, how
come you're going to trade it? How can you trade it for
my sister, and still use it against the bad guys?'

'I'm going to copy it, of course. There's a disc, and
some documents. All I need is to have the folder in my
possession for a few minutes. Then I'll hand over the
originals, but I'll have the evidence. I've persuaded
Kaplan to let the little girl go, if we get the goods. It's
going to work, Alan. Trust me, I know it's going to work.
But listen to me and please believe me, *this is your only
chance.* Three years ago they didn't kill your sister. They
had no reason to kill her. Things are different now. The
missing persons agency story is blown, there's nothing
more to be gained from that charade. It would be better
for NIMROD if Stacey Robarts disappeared again, this
time for ever. Do you understand? I'll tell you what will
happen, if you don't do as I say. The whole operation
here will vanish. You may think you can bring in the
police. It won't do you any good. The flat on the Marina
will be empty. The Arrivals Hall will be a derelict relic of
wartime, there will be no sign that anyone ever stayed at
the Grand Hotel. The site on the Internet will be gone. In
hours, Mr Kaplan will be somewhere else, with another
name and another game. His employers have immense
resources. And Stacey will never be seen again. *Don't you
believe me?*'

'I believe you,' I said. 'That's why I'm here.'

'So you'll do it?'

'I don't understand. If you know where the folder is, why haven't you taken it yourself?'

'Because I can't get near Brennan's house without arousing suspicion. You can.'

'Okay . . .' I frowned. 'So tell me more. What does it look like?'

'It's a dark red plastic document case. About twenty by thirty centimetres, sealed with security tape and stamped with the letters and numbers UAII9544. Don't break the seal, that's very important. I can get it open, copy the stuff and make it look as if it's never been tampered with, but I need to have the folder untouched. It isn't heavy. You'll be able to carry it under your coat. Or in a briefcase if you like. You have a key to the house, and I can give you a copy of the key to the filing cabinet.'

'How did you manage to get that?'

She shook her head. 'It wasn't too difficult. We – my agency – have been on Brennan's case for a while. So will you do it? It's the only way you're going to save your sister.'

'I don't know. This sounds so weird, how can I trust you?'

'Alan, there are things I still can't explain. You'll have to take my word for it that I am on the side of the angels. If I break my cover, three years of vital secret investigation is wasted. Not to mention, I will probably be killed. But *I'm trying to save a child's life.*'

She took off her glasses, and faced me. I had my second surprise. There was no cold calculation in those tawny-grey eyes: only urgency and fear.

I took a deep breath. 'So, I get this folder and bring it to the Marina.'

'When do you think you can get it? It has to be soon.'

'I could do it tomorrow night.'

Jo was coming round to our place. He was taking my mum out to dinner: to make peace after their row, I suspected. I knew that Caz had fixed up to spend the night with a friend. I would have a clear field.

'Good.' She thought for a moment. 'This is what you do. When you have the folder, you bring it to the Marina. Make it around two a.m., when everything should be quiet. There's a boat being repaired, called the *Artemesia II*, on the hard beside the yacht basin. I want you to go to the security light by that boat, stand under it and wait. I'll be on Dittany's houseboat, which is called the *White Heather*. I'll be able to see you. When I see you, I'll go and fetch "Stacey". I won't be long. I'll bring her to you. We'll do the trade.'

'What's *really* behind all this, Demetria? I don't believe in little green men. Or women. What is behind the NIMROD thing? Some kind of industrial espionage? Or is it drugs?'

She stood up. The smile she gave me had no fun in it at all.

'Be honest with yourself, Alan. Do you care?'

I watched her leave the park, walking fast, the wind ruffling her blonde hair.

Could I believe anything she'd told me? Was *Jo Brennan* really on the take? What was this evidence I was to steal from him? How was she going to use it?

It didn't matter. She was right, I didn't care. The only thing that mattered was Stacey.

Jo came round at eight the next evening. They were going out, apparently, to have dinner and see a movie. But it was obvious that there was still trouble between them. The atmosphere was so strained, it reminded me of the time when I first knew that my mum had a boyfriend, and I was angry and jealous and would hardly speak to Jo. Maybe it was lucky things weren't normal, because I don't know how I'd have kept up a cheerful family conversation. But the silence between them was bleak and ominous. It was a relief when they left. I waited a couple of hours, then I caught the bus over to Jo's house. I sat on the top deck thinking, do burglars often travel by bus?

The street was quiet, the house was dark. I let myself in. In my head, as I crept down the well-known hall, with its familiar, seductive feeling of comfort and security, I was rehearsing an explanation: in case Mum and Jo changed their plans and suddenly turned up. My wallet. I'd mislaid my wallet. I thought I might have left it over at Jo's, so I came to have a look . . . Pure nervousness. The curtains in the study were closed. I switched on the desk light. I didn't need Demetria's key. Caz, the little tearaway, had investigated her daddy's 'official business' cabinet ages ago, for the hell of it. She knew where he hid his spare key, in a slot under the top of his desk. I should have told Jo about this, but he'd have been so angry with her. I'd been sure it didn't matter. Jo would never bring anything sensitive away from the office.

Apparently I'd been wrong about that.

I found the folder immediately. It was exactly as Demetria had described it: a slim plastic case with a zip, dark red, sealed and marked with that code. The plastic tape was stamped all over, in big letters: SECURITY – NOT TO BE TAKEN FROM POLICE PREM- ISES. Yet here it was. I hefted it in my gloved hands. I thought about how moody and strange Jo had been over the last weeks. How he'd told me, at the beginning of all this, that he'd investigated NIMROD and they were okay. He'd told me to go along with them, for Mum's sake. But if he'd investigated them at all, surely he must have known that the 'missing persons agency' was a fake . . . I remembered all too clearly how strangely Jo had talked to me, that evening back in May. I remem- bered how unlike himself he'd seemed, the moment NIMROD was mentioned. Was Jo really taking money from criminals?

Which of them should I trust, Jo or Demetria?

I was pretty sure I knew the answer. But not *absolutely* sure.

Demetria was right. If I could get 'Stacey' back, I didn't care what NIMROD was up to, or how much of Demetria's own story didn't add up. Yet that didn't mean I was ready to hand over documents that might, just might, be genuinely important evidence of a weird, huge, scary conspiracy. I wasn't going to leave them here, either. Because Jo might, just might, be working for the bad guys. I'd made up my mind I was going to face him with it. Tell him what Demetria had told me, ask him for an explanation. But I had to get 'Stacey' back first.

I took out the substitute folder I'd brought with me. It looked good. I rifled Jo's desk for office supplies, including a roll of security tape. I knew he was always well equipped. When I'd taped and stamped my folder until it looked as much like the original as possible, I put the real one in a jiffy bag. I sealed it, addressed it to myself, weighed it on Jo's desk scales and stamped it with his franking machine. I knew my deception wouldn't stand up for long. But Demetria wouldn't open the folder straight away. Whether she was really going to copy the contents first, or hand it straight to Mr Kaplan, she'd need to keep the seal unbroken: and she wouldn't be expecting any tricks. She thought she had me well under control.

'*You can tell him another story.*' I remembered Mr Doric Kaplan saying that. Yes, she could always tell me another story when the last one started to unravel.

Not this time.

I glanced around, to be sure that everything in the office looked the way I'd found it, switched off the lamp and slipped out into the hall. Luckily, the weather had turned cool and stormy since the weekend. The thick jacket I was wearing would look normal. I was halfway to the front door, when a shadowy figure materialized out of the gloom in front of me.

The figure reached for a light switch. There was my wannabe kid sister, in bright red pyjamas, her curly hair on end.

'Caz! You're not supposed to be here!'

'I can see that! Alan, *what are you doing*? Why are you acting like a burglar?'

'You're supposed to be sleeping round at your mate's!'

'I decided not to bother. I wasn't in the mood. I'm old enough to stay in the house by myself. I went to bed early, then I heard you creeping about –'

'Caz, *get back to bed*. I swear to you, I'm not doing anything wrong.'

'What have you taken from Dad's study? What's that under your coat? Please don't shut me out, Alan. I want to help you save "Stacey", but you're not doing this right. I'm not a child. I won't let you –'

I'd often felt like strangling Caz, but this was beyond *feeling like*. She was clinging to my arms, looking up at me imploringly. I shook her off. The two folders, the fake one and the real one, dropped from under my jacket. Caz stared at them and at me, eyes big with shock.

I grabbed her and slammed her up against the wall. I was within a millimetre of belting her so hard she would lose teeth. 'Lay off,' I snarled. 'This isn't your business. You're not my sister, you have no right to tell me what to do.'

'I don't want to be your sister,' she whimpered. 'Not if you behave like this. Alan, you're hurting me.'

That fact that I was nearly six foot tall and had muscles was useless to me, except for humping things at work. I never thought about it. But suddenly, now, looking down at Caz, I felt like one of those ugly, nasty, NIMROD heavies.

I let her go. 'Okay, I'm sorry. I'll tell you what I can. I'm going to the Marina. I've got a plan. I'm going to get "Stacey" back. You have to promise me you won't do anything. Not until tomorrow morning. Don't tell anyone you saw me, don't call my mum, or the police or anything. Is that clear?'

'Yes, Alan.' Her timid voice – so unlike bold, bouncy, impossible Caz – made me disgusted with myself. 'I understand. I won't do anything.'

I picked up the folders, let myself out, and hurried off along the dark street.

At a quarter to midnight I was at the Marina. It wasn't raining but the sky was overcast and the wind made the sea roar. The wind rattled in the halyards, in the forest of slender masts. The lights on the dock and the glitter from Beachcombe seafront seemed brighter by contrast with the dark, tumbling clouds. The yacht basin was like a giant aviary, full of the fluttering and whistling of invisible birds.

I seemed to be alone in this concrete and seawater world. I soon located the *Artemesia II*, a biggish sailing boat stuck up on trestles; half covered with a plastic tarpaulin that flapped and showed blue under the tall security light that stood beside it. But I had two hours to play with before Demetria expected me. I calculated where a boat would have to be moored, for me to be visible under that light to someone on board: and spotted what must be Dittany's houseboat. I moved in on it carefully, keeping to the shadows. The *White Heather* had a blue painted hull. The cabin was blue as well, trimmed in white. There were curtains at the windows, and pots of geraniums on deck. There was even a doormat. I sneaked up, keeping out of sight of the brightly lit windows, until I could peer right into the cabin. I saw a little, low-ceilinged room, fussily furnished in chintz with shiny brass fittings. It made me think of the gingerbread house where the witch lived in the fairy tale. There was Dittany. Demetria was with her. There were glasses and a bottle of gin on a table between them. The two women had their heads together, talking like old mates. *Working in deep cover.* I thought bitterly. *On the side of the angels!*

Right. Alan's so dumb he'll believe anything.

I crept away.

I found a place to stand, in deep shadow with my back against the sea wall. I had come here two hours early, because Demetria had said she would leave the houseboat to fetch "Stacey", and it wouldn't take long. My feelings about Demetria was that she told the truth in small things, to make her lies sound better. Therefore, "Stacey" was being kept somewhere near here. But where? On the houseboat? I wondered if I could get on board without alerting those two.

I'd posted the jiffy bag in a pillar box. The fake folder was under my T-shirt, tucked into the waistband of my jeans and belted tight. Soon I might be trading it for my sister's life.

I started to pace up and down, keeping to the shadows. I kept thinking of Demetria's eyes, when she'd taken off her sunglasses at the end of our last interview. I was sure she'd been lying to me all along. Whatever lay behind the NIMROD conspiracy – major drug-smuggling was my best bet – she was in it up to her neck. This folder, the corners of which were digging into my ribs, was what she'd been after from the start. That was clear. Getting the evidence from Jo Brennan's desk had been the whole point of her friendship with me. I didn't blame her for spinning me a line. I'd gone along with her with my eyes open, knowing it was a dangerous game I was playing . . . But she'd never pretended she didn't want anything from me. She'd always said, *I need your help* . . . What if I was wrong? What if she really was a secret agent, working undercover? She'd gone out on a limb, to save my sister's life, and I was planning to betray her. What would Kaplan do when he found out about the switch? How would she talk her way out of that one?

Typically, stupidly, I hadn't thought it through.

My daring plan started to seem incredibly dumb, for all sorts of reasons. It wasn't going to work. Caz was right, I shouldn't have tried to deal with this myself. Poor kid, I hated the way I'd treated her. But that was typical of Alan Robarts. *What if I was wrong?* What if there really was a huge, evil conspiracy, and I was about to wreck the investigation?

I kept glancing towards the *White Heather*, as I wrestled with my problem. The modern pleasure boats on either side towered over it, like skyscrapers crowding a little cottage. A couple of berths along there was a real stunner: a sleek white monster. The length of her hull jutted way beyond the rest. I stared at that raked, gleaming profile, wondering why it seemed familiar. The yacht's name was scribbled in brilliant chrome on the white bows. I could just about read it . . .

It was the *Diamond Life*.

What was she doing here? She should be in her secret berth, safely out of sight.

I felt an exultant grin spreading over my face. My trick must have worked. I'd scrambled the engine-house lock, and stopped them from opening the sea door: long enough for them to miss the tide; and since then the bad weather must have kept them out. Did that mean the cargo was still on board? Then NIMROD was sunk. I could call the police. I could tip them off, as soon as 'Stacey' was safe. Mr Kaplan wouldn't get a chance to find out that the folder was a fake, and it wouldn't matter if he did –

Then I thought of something else: 'Stacey'!

She was somewhere near here. Not on the houseboat, it was too small. Not in the penthouse, Mr Kaplan had abandoned that berth. She had to be on board the *Diamond Life*.

There was nothing moving on deck, as far as I could see. Not a light showing.

Moments later, I stood looking at a gangway between

the yacht and the side of the dock. Nothing but a loop of thick rope barred my way. That, and the man who was suddenly waiting at the top of the gangplank, watching me. I didn't see where he came from. He was just there, all of a sudden: a small, thin guy in dark clothes, with a dark knitted hat pulled down over his forehead. I'd known there would have to be someone on guard. I had a plan. My plan hadn't included the fact that the guard would be carrying a shotgun with the barrel sawn down short. But I wasn't going to give up this chance: and anyway, it was too late to run. I put up my hands, palms outward, and then quickly gave him the NIMROD signs.

I showed him the document case.

'I have to deliver this,' I mouthed, across the space between us.

It worked! He ambled over and unhooked the rope; and beckoned me on board. I was feeling pleased with myself. All I had to do was to tell this goon I had an appointment with Demetria at 2 a.m., convince him to let me wait somewhere; and then start my search. I stepped on to the deck. Immediately, my new friend took my arm. He shoved me aside, and hauled up the gangway. I saw the gleam of his teeth in the dark stubble that covered his skinny jaws. He took the plastic folder from my unresisting hands, stowed it inside his own jacket, and motioned with the shotgun that I was to go ahead of him.

I had the feeling he didn't understand English. Not that it made much difference, I didn't think I could argue my way out of this. I walked ahead. He didn't say a word. He didn't shout to anyone, to report that he'd caught an intruder. This gave me hope. I was now almost sure he was alone on board . . . except for 'Stacey'. We came to a big chest that stood up out of the deck, in the bows. Keeping the barrel of the gun poking at me, he opened the lid, one-handed: and motioned that I was to climb inside. Now I was *sure* he was alone. He was going to lock me in this box for safe keeping, until one of the bosses turned up. I made signs that I wasn't going to get in there. I'd suffocate! He came up close, gesturing angrily with the gun. I had my back to the edge of the chest, frantically wondering if I could vault up, and leap from here to the rail. My hand fastened on something, a loose object lying on top of the heaps of tackle and canvas that almost filled the chest. It felt hard and heavy: some kind of metal rod. Without thinking, I swung it at his head.

The guard dropped to the deck, with hardly a sound.

I was so shocked by this success I nearly yelled aloud. I bent over him to make sure he was still breathing (don't know what I'd have done if he hadn't been), and recovered the fake folder. Then I hauled him up. With some difficulty I got *him* inside the box: shut the lid and bolted it down. I hoped he'd be okay. No one came running, no one shouted.

I dropped the shotgun over the side. Reckoned that was the best place for it.

So here I was, on board the *Diamond Life*; and (for the moment) free to explore.

Somewhere on this ship, I would find my sister. With any luck, I would find out the truth about NIMROD, once and for all.

# Twelve

THE ONLY TIME I'D EVER BEEN ON BOARD A SEA-going ship it was the Channel ferry. I didn't know what to expect. What I found, when I opened the first unlocked door I came to, was chill and silence. There was a dark, empty saloon in the bows, and a passageway towards the stern, with doors on either side. The doors were locked, except for one place that looked like a kitchen, and another that looked like a workshop of some kind. There was no sign of her. But there were so many lockers, bulkheads, hatches: and she might be drugged. If I dared to shout her name she might not hear me. Then there were other levels, above and below. This was going to take some time.

I wished I had a torch. I hadn't thought of bringing one. It wasn't completely dark in here, and I didn't want to risk trying to switch on a light. But the gloom, pallid and luminous from all the white paint, was confusing; and the vague sense of movement under my feet unsettled me. The atmosphere reminded me of those cellars under The Casbah. Something was hinting to me and beckoning me on, towards no good end. *Getting warmer,* whispered the shadows, but this time I wasn't going to like what I would find. Why did I feel so scared? It wasn't like me. *What's the matter with you?* I asked myself. *Are you getting sensible in your old age?* There was a dull humming sound, maybe a generator. The air smelled of carpet glue, seawater, petrol and disinfectant. Its touch on my skin was cloying, as if I was walking through an invisible cold fog. I forced myself to try another door. The handle shifted but wouldn't turn. I was leaning on it, in case it was stiff, not locked, when I heard light footsteps pattering behind me. I whipped around.

She was standing there in the passageway.

'Stacey!'

I had shouted out loud in my amazement. No one came running. The silence was as complete as before. The little girl was gone.

'Stacey!' I shouted again, now confident that we were alone on board. What was she playing at? This was no time for hide-and-seek. If she'd managed to escape from wherever they were keeping her, and she knew I was here, why was she running away? I hurried after her, and found a stairway leading to the upper deck. At the top she was nowhere in sight. Did she think she was being chased by one of the bad guys? Ahead of me were double doors of pebble-thick glass in small squares, framed in varnished wood and gleaming brass. 'Stacey! It's me, Alan. I've come to rescue you again –'

Then she was there, in front of me. In my mind's eye, projected on the half-darkness. My sister Stacey. Not NIMROD's Stacey, but my dead sister as she had haunted me, in her blue shorts with the yellow daisies, in her dolphin T-shirt. Her blonde hair lay wet and darkened in tangles on her shoulders; her feet were bare. I recoiled, I staggered back against the wall of the stairway. I didn't know if my eyes were open or closed. It didn't matter. This is what it means to see a ghost. It isn't an object or an image in the outside world. It's something that happens, where everything important happens to you: in your mind.

I had fallen to my knees. I was crouching on the stairs, my hands over my face. Sick and shuddering. I managed to take them away. The ghost was gone. I stood up, and went towards the double doors. Somewhere on this boat there was a small girl locked up: a strange, brave, bewildered little girl without a past. She was relying on me, and I must find her quickly. But just now, I had another appointment. The hair stood on the nape of my neck. I was shaking with helpless dread. I must go to meet my sister.

The doors weren't locked. It was another saloon the same as on the deck below, but smaller and more luxurious. There was soft carpet on the floor, windows all around, a kidney-shaped cocktail bar in one corner. I could smell tobacco smoke: Mr Kaplan's brand of cigars. There were lockers running along the walls, under the level of the windows. I began to open them. The first two were empty, apart from some ashtrays, corkscrews and glasses. The third was locked, a chunky ordinary lock on which Demetria's gadget could have made no impression. I searched around. Behind the cocktail bar I found some handyman tools on a shelf. I took a big screwdriver, returned to the locked doors and applied it ruthlessly. Inside the cupboard there was a portable cassette player – nothing high tech, just an ordinary make – and some boxes full of tape cassettes. I sat on the floor and examined them. The boxes were unmarked. Each cassette had a handwritten label with a date on it. The dates were close together. I guessed they must tell when these recordings were made.

Three years ago.

In July and August, in the summer when Stacey disappeared.

I pulled out a cassette at random, and stuck it in the machine. Maybe the batteries would be dead. No. The tape went around, there was a hiss: then voices. An adult voice asking questions, calm and quiet. A boy's voice, answering. I listened . . .

I stopped the tape, chucked it out and tried another.

I kept on doing this: listening for a few moments, then throwing out the tape, until I was surrounded by a litter of cassettes. One of them held me for longer than the others . . .

*'She was saying hepup, hepup, we're in the fortune factory –'*

*'You mean, help help? She was calling for help?'*

*'She used to say hepup when she meant help. But she wasn't calling for help. She trusted me. She was being brilliant. It was a joke. You see, last Christmas when we were pulling crackers I told that old joke about the Chinese fortune cookie, you know those crispy twists of biscuit, and when you break it there's a bit of paper inside with your fortune on it. Well, this guy opened his cookie, and instead of a fortune there was a message: Help! I'm being held prisoner in a Chinese Fortune Cookie Factory. Stacey loved that, she kept on saying the punch line for ages, but she didn't understand it and she kept on getting it wrong.'*

*'So she wasn't calling for help? You hadn't done anything to frighten her?'*

*'No! Stacey's never frightened. She used to say that too. 'I'm NEVER frightened'. She meant we were stuck. But we weren't, because there was the path up the cliff. The sunbather told us where it was, and it was there –'*

*'I don't understand about the "fortune factory", Alan. Could you explain that to me again?'*

He tried to explain, but he was crying too hard. They had asked so many questions, over and over again. Some that made sense and plenty that didn't, because they didn't know what to believe. Because this boy had lied. He had lied for weeks about what happened the day his sister vanished. He'd hidden her bag and the clothes he'd been wearing. Now they wanted to know every single thing that he remembered about Stacey, because they didn't know what else he might be hiding. He told them everything. He babbled and told them so much, more than he could possibly remember about afterwards –

So now I understood how NIMROD's hostage had

known things I thought only the real Stacey could know. Now I knew how NIMROD had managed their cruel deception. It was poetic justice. It was me, I did it . . . I sat there listening to my own voice, my voice when I was thirteen. It was like turning the pages of a photograph album. Pictures appeared in my head, of forgotten scenes. The kind, grey-haired social-worker lady, the fat police-woman with the worried smile, the policeman with the glasses who always sat there in the background, typing. I knew I was under suspicion and I was scared. But underneath the fear there was such an emptiness. Nothing I could say would bring her back, nothing would undo what I had done –

My eyes dazzled. She was so young.

Better a millstone be tied round his neck, and he be thrown into the deep . . . I remembered those words, didn't know from where. But he was right, whoever said that. I'd rather die than go on living, knowing what I'd done. They said it wasn't my fault, but they were wrong –

There was a sound of pattering bare feet, a scuffling leap, and a warm, solid body hit me right in the chest.

'My Alan! I knew you'd come!'

'Stacey' – the living 'Stacey', the NIMROD gang's imposter – was clinging to me like a monkey. 'They shut me in a cabin,' she cried. 'When the aliens grabbed me from your friend's flat, this is where they brought me. They've been stuck here because of what you did, you made them really mad! I've been locked up. But they didn't know that I could get out of the little window into the passage. I heard you calling, I wriggled and wriggled, and I got out!'

She looked at the cassette player, and her grin faded. 'Who's that? Why is he crying?'

I got to my feet, shedding the kid. I switched the machine off.

'No one you need worry about. Come on.'

But I'd been listening to those tapes for too long.

Before we reached the doors of the saloon, someone stepped through them and switched on the lights.

'I'm sorry,' said Demetria, looking at the litter of cassettes around the player. 'I'm sorry you had to find out like this, Alan.'

We looked at each other, across the gap that couldn't be bridged. No more stories now.

'How did you get hold of the tapes?'

'You really don't know, do you? It proves there's nothing disguises you like a uniform. But you didn't see me, back then, unless we happened to pass each other in a corridor. Otherwise I wouldn't have dared to come near you, not even in civvies with my hair a different colour. As it was, I didn't dare go near your mother. Or Jo, of course. I couldn't go near Jo Brennan.'

'You were in the police? But how could you be? You were my sunbather.'

'I was both, Alan. I was WDC Angela Wallace, but I was on the sea defences that day, working for my *other* employer. I want to explain, Alan. I want you to understand . . . When I was a little girl, I was always a handful. My dad used to say, you'll always be on the side of at least one of the angels . . . His little joke. I was in the police and I was working for Kaplan too. I was already in deep. His name's not really Kaplan, by the way: and if you tried, you'd find it very hard to link him to Kaplan Communications.' She was walking towards me as she spoke. 'You have the little girl, even if she's not your Stacey. Did you bring the file? Will you give it to me? Please, Alan.' She reached out. 'We've been friends, haven't we? Save my life.'

'First tell me what it's all about. The truth, this time.'

'Don't be stupid!' shouted 'Stacey'. 'You don't have to give her anything. I already *told* you what it's all about. It's *aliens*. I'll *show* you!'

She darted away, zoomed past Demetria and vanished into the darkness.

# Thirteen

'STACEY' RAN, I RACED AFTER HER. I DIDN'T DARE to call out, in case Demetria had not come on board alone. But the kid had the wrong idea. When she reached the main deck she kept on going down. I had to follow: through a hatchway, down another steep flight of steps, along another passage where it was almost pitch dark and the stink of fuel was mixed with other foul smells. 'Stacey!' I shouted. 'Come back! We have to get off this boat! Where are you going? This isn't the way!'

She didn't pay any attention to me. She'd stopped because there was nowhere left to run, when I almost fell over her. By the light of a dull lamp set above it, she was working at the door that must lead into the *Diamond Life*'s hold.

'Open it, Alan! Then you'll see!'

I struggled to lift a heavy bar that was slotted in place behind a row of bolts. 'Stacey' pushed the doors . . . I saw eyes, glimmering at me. It seemed like hundreds of eyes.

There was a foul smell. I couldn't see their faces. They didn't look human. They moved, but it didn't look like human movement, more like a tide of cockroaches in a dirty kitchen, disturbed by a sudden light. So this was the mysterious cargo that should have been unloaded two days ago. My God, I thought. She was telling the truth all along.

*Aliens*.

'You see,' declared 'Stacey' triumphantly. 'I *told* you.'

Then my mind cleared, my eyes caught up with

themselves. I saw that the ballast hold of the *Diamond Life* was packed with nothing stranger than a crowd of utterly miserable human beings. They must have been locked in here at least since Saturday night. From the smell, there were no sanitary arrangements: and a lot of people had been sick at some point in their rough weekend, as well as needing the toilet. They seemed mostly young men, some older men and a few women. Some of them were clutching bundles of possessions, all of them looked half dead. So this was the big secret.

They were aliens all right. They were illegal immigrants.

I just stared, open-mouthed.

'It was like this,' said Demetria's voice behind me. 'Jo Brennan had been sniffing around Lenny for years. It wasn't a problem. Lenny – you know him as Mr Doric Kaplan – wasn't going to get nicked. He's too big for that. You saw the flat, and that's just temporary accommodation while he was sorting out this gig. He has better places than that, all over the world. But he doesn't like interference. He decided he was going to bring Jo Brennan down. We looked for Brennan's weak point, and it was obvious: his girlfriend, Jackie Robarts, and her obsession with little lost Stacey. So then we looked for a child who could stand in for Stacey. When we'd found her we brought her down here, installed her in the Arrivals Hall, and trained her. I'd been able to get hold of copies of the interview tapes – same source as I got my copy of the key to Jo Brennan's filing cabinet. I still have contacts in the police. It was poetic justice. The way Stacey vanished, right next door to the Arrivals Hall, could have made things very awkward for our immigration business, back then. It caused us real problems for a while even as it was: with the police search, and the divers all over the place. They didn't find anything, but Lenny remembers things like that.

'So we were settling an old score with the Robarts

family, and destroying Jo Brennan as well. That was enough to make it worthwhile, even though it took a long time and a lot of work to get everything just right. Dittany trained the kid and handled your mum. My job was to keep you distracted. Lenny was in charge of the movies, director and producer. He enjoyed that. He loves making movies. He gets the latest equipment, stuff that's not on the market yet, from friends of his in Germany and Japan. That's what he wants to do, you know. He's getting out of crime. He wants to make sci-fi movies. Real ones, in Hollywood. He's going to give me a chance there too. I'm going to act. It's what I've always wanted.'

I turned, wrenching myself with difficulty from the grip of all those eyes. Demetria was standing at the bottom of the narrow stairway, gripping 'Stacey' by the arm.

'Where do they come from? There's a bigger ship. It's called the *Nimrod*, if you're interested.' She grinned. 'It appealed to Lenny to use the name. It worked well, didn't it: all that tosh about Nimrod the mighty hunter? And the signs. (Actually, we've no idea what those signs mean. It's something the customers made up, so they'd know each other. Illegal immigrants have to be careful who they talk to. But we took them over, to add a bit more convincing detail to the routine.) Passwords, mystery, secret meetings: people like your mum love that stuff. Anyway . . . Nimrod brings them to the Threshers, those rocks you call "The Islands". They transfer on to the *Diamond Life*. We land them, set them up with English clothes, some kind of papers and smuggle them into their new lives. They usually can't pay much when they book their passage, but we get them jobs and they pay the rest off gradually. There are plenty of employers who rely on us for cheap labour, no questions asked. It's like the old smuggling days, it's romantic really. We're doing these people a big favour.'

'You mean, they think they're buying the diamond life, and when they get here they find they're practically slaves,' I said, bitterly. 'Only you do better. The old slavers never thought of getting the slaves to pay for their own tickets.'

'Whatever. It's getting less profitable anyway. Lenny was almost ready to pull out. The plan was, as soon as we'd suckered Brennan, and arranged for him to be exposed as a bent copper, we'd fold everything and walk away. So it didn't matter much if a few of our business secrets were exposed –'

'But Jo knew NIMROD was a fake! He didn't fall for it, I know he didn't.'

She laughed. 'We never expected him to. It was your mum we had to convince. And your mum, well, if you're desperate you'll believe anything. Isn't that right, Alan? Jo Brennan likes to live in style. He's not reckless but he spends every penny he earns. We knew he didn't have any spare cash. So when your mum came to him asking for money, that she had to have *at once*, we knew he'd be in trouble. And she had to come to him, because . . . You don't know what we were asking for those sessions. It was a lot of money, a real lot. *That* was how we got him. Jo needed cash, very urgently, and we had made sure that he already knew where cash could be had. He couldn't stand to lose your mother. He couldn't refuse to pay for her to get her baby back. It was a peach. Soon we had videos of him taking money, from a known criminal. When he knew we had those, he had to do whatever we asked.'

'I don't believe it!'

She shrugged. 'You can believe what you like. But he was ready to co-operate –'

'Except that he changed his mind.' I remembered Jo's strange attitude to NIMROD, and then the way he'd clasped my hand, that night in his study, and promised me: *I won't let you down.* 'He changed his mind. He refused to be blackmailed. *That*'s why you needed me.'

Still nobody had moved in the hold. I could feel all those eyes staring at my back. But I couldn't take my own eyes off Demetria. One hand, her left hand, gripped 'Stacey'. The other hand had taken something from the pocket of her dark jacket. It was a gun. It looked like one I'd seen the night we 'broke into' Mr Kaplan's penthouse. The small muzzle was pointing straight at me. I couldn't see the expression in her tawny-grey eyes, but I knew how she was feeling. We were so alike. She'd always been a bit wild. Right and wrong had never seemed to matter much, as long as she was having fun. But now the game had gone too far, and she couldn't see how to turn back.

'I knew she wasn't on our side,' cried 'Stacey'. 'You said she was, but I knew she wasn't.'

'Why did you help me to escape?' I asked, trying to keep absolutely still. 'That's one of the things that puzzled me. Letting me go wasn't part of Kaplan's plan. I know it wasn't. I was supposed to be taken out to sea and chucked overboard.' Actually, I couldn't care less why she'd helped me, but anything to keep her talking –

'I didn't want them to kill you, Alan!' she cried. 'I *like* you. I liked you from the start. We had fun together, didn't we? That time when we invaded his flat? That was great, scary but great: playing with Big Daddy's things, do you remember how he looked, standing there in the middle of that mayhem? He knew I was going to pretend to break in and all that, but he didn't know I was going to go berserk . . . The best fun. So I left you my unilock. You should have shut the cell door again, then you'd have had a bit more time . . . When he found her gone, I couldn't stop him from sending the heavies to get "Stacey" back. But I meant to keep our bargain, Alan. I swear I did. *I was trying to save the kid's life.* Only now it's no good. You shouldn't have come on board the *Diamond Life*, you shouldn't have found those tapes. I'm sorry, Alan. I'm truly sorry, but now I have to look out for myself –'

'You saw my sister fall.'

*'There was nothing I could do!'* Her voice rose in a wail.

'Yes, okay, maybe I saw her fall. But what could I do? I couldn't do anything for her, she was surely dead, I had to get out of there. Or they'd have found the *Diamond Life*'s berth and it would have been my fault, I'd have been done for, everything would have fallen apart. Give me the folder, Alan!'

I pulled the fake folder out of my waistband. 'You wouldn't shoot me. That's murder.'

I saw her eyes flicker, but her voice stayed hard. 'So? Lenny's tough on troublemakers. You wouldn't be the first human casualty in the NIMROD business, believe me. I'm going to come out of this okay, Alan. No matter what.' The hand that held the gun was steady. My lost witness had finally told me the truth: the truth about Stacey, the truth about herself. I heard the fear and determination that was my death sentence –

I made as if to hold the folder out to her. Instead I turned and threw it into the hold, into the silence of those helpless watching faces. I had tried, in the split second before I made my move, to give 'Stacey' a warning glance. She was brilliant, that kid. She twisted around and bit Demetria-Angela's wrist: a good hard chomp. Demetria yelled, lost her grip, and lunged forward, trying to grab the case before it hit the floor. 'Stacey' ran.

I pelted up the stairs after the little girl: and out on to the deck. I gasped a great lungful of fresh air. It had started to rain, I felt the drops whipped by the wind, smacking me in the face. Then I heard 'Stacey' yelling 'Alan, get back!' Demetria-Angela had brought company, or else Mr Kaplan had sent reinforcements to find out what she was doing. The yacht seemed to be alive with dark figures. There was something happening on the dockside too. I saw headlights and heard sirens, but I didn't take it in, I thought it was part of the ambush: more bad guys. We had to get to the gangplank. I shouted this to 'Stacey', but she didn't have a chance to obey me. She was running around the deck, evading one heavy after another, screaming at the top of her voice. I knocked over one guy, just by barrelling into him. 'Stacey' had managed to get up on the rail, on the seaward side. Three big men had closed round her in a semicircle. 'Leave her alone,' I shouted. 'It's over, she's no use to you, everyone knows she's not my sister –' But they didn't understand English, or it was no good anyway. The next time I looked, 'Stacey' had disappeared.

'Stace!' I yelled. 'You can't swim!'

I raced, hauling off my jacket. I vaulted up: and I was there, on the brink, looking down. It was night instead of daylight, cold rain instead of sunlight. I have always been afraid of deep water. If I could have made myself jump into that blank blue abyss, I might have found her. Stacey might be alive today –

I leapt. Didn't even try to dive. I fell like a stone, landed feet first with an almighty smack and went straight under, a long way. The cold water churned, full of light and darkness, the white flank of the *Diamond Life* bore down on me. I came up choking, shouting 'Stacey! Stacey!' I couldn't see her, I couldn't see anything. I forgot how to tread water and went down again, shouting in panic . . .

Luckily for 'Stacey' other people had seen what happened and they'd come rushing to the rescue. The third time I broke the surface a pair of big hands grabbed me. I tried to fight them, but a gruff voice growled, 'Lay off, son, I'm on your side'. There were more hands, hauling me up: I was in a harbour launch. I tried to dive over the side again. A woman in a life jacket and coastguard uniform grabbed me. 'She's okay. She's out, already, she's fine.'

'She's not fine! She's dead, she's dead. You can't fool me this time. I saw her fall –'

Next thing I remember I was on the dock, spewing pints of seawater and crying helplessly. Someone flung a blanket round me, I tried to throw it off –

'Are you all right, my Alan?'

'Stacey,' NIMROD's 'Stacey', was standing there dripping, wrapped in her own blanket, eyes like saucers. 'Oh, my Alan,' cried the brave little stranger with my sister's name. 'You saved my life!'

Things gradually started to get less confused. I saw that there was an ambulance on the dock, and several police cars. The coastguards seemed to be out in force as well. They were all over the *Diamond Life* and the *White Heather*. People from Marina Apartments and from the moored houseboats had emerged into the rain. They stared at the show from behind a line of constables, as Mr Doric Kaplan and his small army were parcelled out into the cars.

'I'm sorry, Alan,' said Caz, swimming into view of my blurry, salt-stung eyes. 'I didn't wait. I dialled 999 and called everyone I could think of, soon as you left me. I *had* to.'

Then Jo came up. Beside him was another man, a thin man with steel-framed glasses. They were wearing raincoats. The thin man was smiling, but Jo looked grim. I thought he'd been arrested. 'Jo,' I gasped, still full of the terrible news Demetria had given me. 'Are you in trouble? What can I do, how can I help? I know you didn't –' Then I gaped at them, horrified that I'd said too much.

'Don't worry, Alan,' said the thin man. 'The situation's under control. Everything will be explained later. Now let's get you home.'

Jo wrapped me, wet blanket and all, in a bear hug. 'Thank God you're all right,' he groaned. 'I blame myself, I should have thought of some way to warn you, Alan. But I had to tell Jackie and get her to understand. That was hard enough, and the fewer people who knew, the better. It's okay, it's all right. No one is in trouble tonight – that doesn't well deserve to be.'

It was all spinning. The lights, the darkness, the sirens. Somewhere near to me, Demetria was being taken away, disarmed: her wild game over. The Grand Hotel would close down, there would be no more cargoes delivered to the Arrivals Hall. Caz was hanging on to my arm, 'Stacey' was squeezing my hand in her wet little mitt, they were coming with me to a police car. My mum was there, putting her arms round me, crying and smiling at once.

Something was over. Finally, for ever. It was time to begin again.

# *Fourteen*

*I* LEFT STACEY SITTING AGAINST THE CLIFF,
  perfectly safe, then I went round the corner. The path
the sunbather had told us about was easy. In a few
minutes I was on the top of Beachcombe cliffs. I turned a
few cartwheels and I hurried back. When I got to the
corner I had a terrible shock. *Stacey was gone!* I cried out
her name, lost my footing and landed with a crash. I must
have knocked myself out for a moment. In those few
seconds a whole long horrible nightmare went through
my head. Stacey was dead, the police thought I'd
murdered her, my dad moved away, I failed all my exams.
My mum became a grief-stricken robot and so did I, until
one day our dreary existence turned into a kind of thriller,
with guns, plots, secret passageways, blackmail, burglary,
weird bad guys: but none of it was any fun, because
Stacey was still dead and gone.

Then I woke up from this awful dream, and I heard her
calling me. She hadn't fallen into the sea, she hadn't
broken her neck. She'd tried to follow me, and slipped
down between two of the concrete knucklebones. Well, I
hauled her out and I yelled at her, because I'd told her to
stay put. But it's never any good yelling at our Stacey, so I
soon gave that up. I was too glad she was alive to be really
angry. Our friendly sunbather had gone, I don't know
where. No sign of that motor yacht I thought I saw,
either.

We climbed up on to the clifftop, no problem. I
searched the pockets of my soaking wet shorts again, and

I found a little soaked lump of paper that turned out to be a fiver, folded up small, that I'd forgotten about. So I treated us both to White Magnums, from the kiosk at the end of the esplanade. We lay on the sea wall there, eating them and drying off in the afternoon sun: me weak with relief, and vowing I would never, ever again take a risk or do anything remotely dodgy. Then we went home, using the rest of the fiver for bus fares.

Tired but happy.

Nah.

Can't turn back the hand of time.

It's strange to think that all the time Demetria, Doric and Dittany were playing their trick on Mum and me, Jo Brennan's office was working its own sting on Lenny Bross, a rich businessman with a lot of shady interests. They knew his money was ultimately coming from organized crime, but they'd never been able to stick anything on him, he was too good at keeping his hands clean. But when Lenny decided to bring down Jo Brennan, he got carried away with his own artistry, and that's the way they trapped him. Jo did take the money, just the way Demetria told me: but he was only pretending. All the while, the police were gathering their own evidence, and (until that spectacular night on the Marina) what finally put the finger on Lenny was that they could prove he'd set up those payments. It was Lenny, not Jo, who was caught out. Jo talked to me about his part in this affair. He didn't like what he had to do, pretending to take money. He didn't like busting the illegal immigrants racket either. There was a moral dilemma for everyone there, said Jo: because whatever happens to the criminals, the passengers suffer as well. He'd found it specially hard, because his own mum and dad had been immigrants. But in the end, he said, you have to stop the slavers. Because, just as I said when I saw them, on board the *Diamond Life*, that's what Lenny's operation was. A slave trade.

I asked him, wasn't he even tempted. When Mum was insisting that the little girl really was Stacey, and swearing she'd never speak to him again if his sting on Lenny meant she lost contact with her baby? Wasn't he tempted not to tell them at the office, and just play along? He said no. 'I don't make mistakes like that,' he told me. 'I have too much to lose. I have my lover, and my daughter, and a young man I would be proud to call my son. I want them to be proud of me, always.'

'But what if it really *had been* Stacey? There was always that chance –'

'Oh, Alan,' he said, when I asked him that. He shook his head at me, sadly.

He was right. There had never been that chance. In my heart, I think I'd known it all along. Even on the night when I was most certain that I'd found my sister . . .

We think the living 'Stacey', NIMROD's 'Stacey', is a Romany child. From the few words we've got her to remember of her own language, she's probably from the Czech Republic. According to Chairman Williams, the woman we knew as 'Dittany', she came to England with her father (her mother being dead) on the *Nimrod* the year our Stacey disappeared. The father abandoned his kid and Charmain, to avoid trouble, found a foster home for her with a family that owed Lenny favours. There she stayed, until she was spotted as a Stacey Robarts lookalike, when Lenny was looking for a way to ruin Jo Brennan's life. We think that she remembers more than she'll admit, but she won't say much. She's still very scared about things that happened to her, back then. So we don't know any more details, yet. We haven't managed to trace any relatives, and we don't know how much of Charmain's story is true. But it could be that the young man whose decomposed body the police found, walled up in the cellar under The Casbah, in the room Caz and I thought was haunted, will turn out to have been her father. Lenny, as Demetria warned me, had a tough way with troublemakers.

There's not much doubt that they were going to kill her too. She'd seen 'Doric Kaplan', she knew about the 'cargoes'. She was a danger to Lenny. They were going to kill her, as soon as she was no further use to them. And she knew it, poor kid. She might talk, childishly, about 'aliens from outer space': but she knew exactly what kind of monsters were holding her prisoner.

For the moment she lives with Mum and me and Jo and Caz. She's not as easy to handle as she was when the adventure was going on. She lies, she steals, she won't go to school. She's a very angry little girl at times . . . But it's okay. We're getting there. Mum says that once, before the years when she was ill-treated, she must have been loved. Because at the back of everything, she has this basic ability to trust. It makes her reachable. If all attempts to trace her relatives fail, Mum and Jo are planning to adopt her, if they're allowed.

She still insists Torquil's always been hers. But Angela Wallace says she picked the cyberpet up on the sea defences the day she saw my sister fall. She took it into the Arrivals Hall and forgot about it. Eventually she found it again, and they used it as a prop when they were training their 'Stacey'. After Angela-Demetria's statement, the police were ready to send down more divers to look for my sister's body. But Mum and Dad said no and I agreed with them. It doesn't matter any more. It's time to let go.

I have nothing but contempt for Doric and Dittany. I feel differently about Demetria. I know she lied to me, I know she was as much a villain as the others, I know she panicked and would have shot me at the end, but I believe she really was trying to save Stacey's life. Not only when she offered me that deal, but all through the adventure. She knew Lenny planned to kill off his little imposter. Maybe, like me, she was haunted by the memory of that summer's day, when another little girl had died, and Demetria did nothing to save her. And so – selling the idea to Lenny as a cunning diversion – she did her devious best to get the kid rescued. She came to me, out of the past that bound us together, and offered us both a second chance.

No matter what happened later, I have to be grateful for that.

Besides, unlike Jo Brennan, I know how it feels to take that first dodgy step. When I think of her, I see someone very like myself. Someone who started out taking a little risky extra cash, for the thrill of it as much as anything: and ended up in that stinking hold, pulling a gun on a teenager and a child. Maybe that's her gift to me, a christening gift from a bent-out-of-shape fairy god-mother, for my new beginning. As long as I live I hope I always remember how easy it is to be tempted, how easy it is to fall: and how ugly the place you find yourself, once you tumble over that brink.

So here I am again on the concrete knucklebones, with the murmuring waves below me, on a warm hazy day in October. We're moving right away from Beachcombe. It's the sensible thing to do. I'll get another job, I hope. Who knows, I might really get into Retail Trainee Management. It'd be a shame to waste all that customer-profile studying I did for Big Liz. I'll miss Mo Doyle. I'll miss my other mates at Countryfare, even Big Liz herself. I'll miss this too, the sun and the air: the cliffs and the sea and the wide open sky. Maybe, one day, I'll come back. But it won't be for years. It's best to make a long, clean break.

The sun's going down. It's time to head home.

Goodbye, Stacey, sleep well.

Other books by Ann Halam

## The Powerhouse

*'The face looked at Maddy. I saw its empty eyes gleam . . .*
*Somebody screamed and screamed. I think it was me.'*
Robs, Jef and Maddy: three friends who just wanted to
make music together. How could one summer change
their lives the way it did? Maddy and Robs survived, but
only just, and the nightmare that happened in the
Powerhouse will live with them for ever.

'superbly packaged horror'   *Books Magazine*

'worth twenty Point Horrors'   *School Librarian*

## The Fear Man

A dreadful secret hangs over the house in Roman Road.
What is it that keeps drawing Andrei to it? And what is
the unknown presence that seems to be stalking the
family? Constantly on the run from a father he has never
known, Andrei is living a nightmare. A compelling story
of vampires, magicians and creatures of darkness.

'brilliantly written . . . a very powerful and affecting book'
*BBC Radio 4 Treasure Islands*

## The Haunting of Jessica Raven

*'Darkness. A cold, foul-smelling darkness. Somewhere a child was screaming.'*

Mysterious things start happening to Jessica when, on holiday in France, she meets a strange group of ragged children. She cannot work out where they come from, but when she meets their leader, an older boy called Jean-Luc, she begins to realize that they may hold the key to her brother's fatal illness.

'a novel of singular completeness and perfection. With it Ann Halam confirms her standing as one of the most exciting of emerging talents' *Junior Bookshelf*

## Crying in the Dark

*'She didn't know why she had such a strange feeling that they shouldn't have left her alone – but suddenly she understood what the ghosts were trying to tell her. She could make the Madisons wish they'd never been born . . .'*

Bullied and abused by her adoptive family Elinor retreats into the restless, vengeful past that haunts their seventeenth-century home. At first it's a way to escape, but soon she's a prisoner and the price of her freedom is something too terrible to contemplate.

'an excellent and compelling ghost story . . .' *The Guardian*